Horse Healer

Starlight

D1355623

Also available in this series:

Eclipse
Puzzle
Sapphire

Horse Healer

Starlight

Judy Waite

SCHOLASTIC

For Andy

Scholastic Children's Books,
Commonwealth House, 1–19 New Oxford Street
London WC1A 1NU, UK
a division of Scholastic Ltd
London ~ New York ~ Toronto ~ Sydney ~ Auckland
Mexico City ~ New Delhi ~ Hong Kong

First published by Scholastic Ltd, 2000

Copyright © Judy Waite, 2000

ISBN 0 439 01290 2

Typeset by
Cambrian Typesetters, Frimley, Camberley, Surrey
Printed by Mackays of Chatham plc

2 4 6 8 10 9 7 5 3 1

Author's Note

Writing *Starlight* gave me the chance to do some exciting research. Not only did I have to keep learning about Gypsies and horses – I also had to find out as much as I could about the film world.

I read as much as I could, made lots of phone calls, and spent a brilliant day out on a BBC film set, talking to directors, film crew, extras – and anyone else who could spare the time to talk to me. I met lots of great people, and would especially like to thank:

Marilyn Fox – a script writer and script "doctor".

Alison Law, one of the directors for the BBC television series "Casualty".

Sue Summerskill, a licensed child chaperone.

All these people helped the background detail in the story "come alive".

Starlight is also the final piece of work for a college course that I have been doing, studying for an MA in Creative Writing for Children at King Alfred's College, Winchester.

1

Nicky heard the horse before he saw her. He turned quickly as she burst through a jagged break in the hedge, cantered down a crumbling row of old stone steps, and raced across the field towards him.

She was light chestnut – the colour of spun gold – her silvery tail trailing like a comet behind her.

An explosion of thoughts flashed through Nicky's mind. The horse was riderless, her reins and stirrups flapping wildly as she moved. She had come from the grounds of Chestnut Court, but Chestnut Court was a dangerous place, a crumbling manor house due for demolition. Who had been riding this horse round there? And what had happened to them now?

The horse wasn't local – Nicky knew all the horses that lived nearby and this silky gold creature would have stuck in his mind. And yet – there was something about her – something familiar...

The horse was still galloping. Nicky could hear her snorts now. See the foam from her mouth. The whites of her eyes. He pulled his thoughts together. She was heading straight for him – him and the tree that he'd been walking away from, kicking his way through the conkers and fallen leaves.

Nicky decided to stand his ground. That way she would have to swerve round him, away from the lowest spread of branches. *And* it would give him more chance to make contact.

He let her come nearer, her hooves throwing up clouds of dust and stones as she thundered on.

And it was then that Nicky saw two things that hit him like a rock in the stomach. There were blood specks on her neck and shoulders – and she wasn't riderless at all. Bouncing and bumping on the side furthest away from Nicky, one foot twisted awkwardly in the stirrup, someone was being dragged along the ground.

Suddenly there was no time for anything but action.

Nicky leaped forward, making a desperate grab at the horse's reins.

2

2

Strangely, the horse didn't fight him.

She stopped immediately, her dark eyes watching him carefully.

"Steady," Nicky spoke softly, raising his hand to stroke her. But as his fingers brushed her neck he realized he was shaking all over, his insides churning as if they'd just gone through a liquidizer. He dropped his hand away quickly. Nicky knew horses. He knew all the ways to touch them. Their deepest thoughts. Their secret language. And he knew too that if he touched her while he felt like this, he risked his own shock striking into her, sending her hurtling away again.

And the fallen rider on the other side wasn't moving. This was no time for taking chances.

Nicky shifted his body slightly, turning his eyes away from the horse. He knew a direct stare could seem like a threat. A Big Cat fixing on its prey. Nicky edged his way very slowly, moving round to the other side.

It was a child – Nicky couldn't tell the age. Its foot was still twisted in the stirrup and it swayed awkwardly upside down. Dressed in jeans and a checked shirt, its blond hair was tangled with leaves and twigs and bits of grass.

Nicky felt the sting of bile catch in his throat. He fought back a rush of panic, trying to remember the first aid lesson from a Red Cross woman at school last term.

"Whaddya think you're doing?"

Nicky jumped, shaking his head in silent warning at the sun-blond boy who appeared suddenly behind him. "There's someone really hurt. They're not moving or anything. I think they might be..."

The boy ducked under the horse's head, leaning against her and watching Nicky through turquoise-blue eyes.

"Come on," Nicky hissed a in whisper. "Give me a hand."

"You might have ruined hours of work." The boy sounded part bored, part amused. His voice was husky. An American drawl. He was making no effort to whisper back.

Confusion brought a dark flush to Nicky's tanned face and his green eyes flashed. "What are you talking about?"

The boy shrugged, pushing back the long floppy fringe that fell sideways over his forehead. "Take another look."

Nicky turned again to the child, and then pushed his knuckles hard against his mouth, trying not to cry out. Its head had twisted round, the eyes blank and staring. And the truth ripped through him like stone through cloth. It wasn't a child – not a real child – just a soft foam dummy, dressed in the same jeans and checked shirt as the boy, its foot tied with string and knotted on to the stirrup.

Nicky turned, moving in slow motion, and stared at the blood along the horse's neck. Except it wasn't real blood either. Nicky could see that now. Just a red spray of some kind. He looked back at the boy. "How was I to know..."

"I've been practising." The boy flicked his thumb towards Chestnut Court. "The film crew are lining things up to do the real take tomorrow. I was working the horse on my own for a while. I needed to check that it knew what it was doing. If I haven't got it right by sunset everyone's going to be really ticked off with you."

Nicky's eyes followed the direction of the boy's thumb.

Nicky had poked around Chestnut Court before of course. He'd been with Billy Clarke, a boy from school. Billy had gone right inside, and come back stammering about cellars and tunnels, but Nicky had only looked round the grounds and peered in the windows a bit. A stately home caving in on his head hadn't been his idea of a good time. And what he'd seen hadn't made him want to search further. It was just a crumbling shell of a building. Anything valuable or special about it was long gone. But once upon a time Chestnut Court had been beautiful. Built on a steep bank, raised above the fields and surrounding countryside, it had been a royal retreat. Now, with its pale amber walls lit gold beneath the late afternoon sun, it seemed suddenly touched with the echoes of what it had once been. It looked magical. Unreal. A fairy-tale palace.

As he scanned the building, Nicky saw a swift movement out of the corner of his eye. A figure – a woman in a purple dress – stepped out from behind one of the stone pillars. She wasn't alone – something was moving with her, something dark and shadowy. Nicky squinted, trying to work it out, but she dipped out of sight down some steep stone steps and disappeared from view.

At the same time Nicky heard a shout. Between the gap in the hedge a cluster of people were hovering. People pointing cameras. People wearing head-phones. People carrying pads and pens.

Suddenly everything clicked. Nicky turned back to the boy. "Oh hell. I know who you are. You're filming here aren't you?"

"Trying to."

"There's been a rumour at school about you lot coming, but no one knew exactly where or when."

"That was the way we wanted it."

Nicky hesitated. He wanted to go. He wasn't comfortable with this slim boy with his chiselled features and sky-bright eyes. And he wasn't interested in film stuff. He'd never even been to the cinema. But if he left now, there was someone who might never forgive him. "Sabrina – my sister – has been on about this film for ages. She's nuts about that Levi Buick bloke. She says..." He paused again, the possibility dawning slowly. "You're not – you can't be—" Nicky stared at him, his mouth hanging open.

Levi Buick raised one thick, heavy eyebrow very slightly, and folded his arms.

Nicky pushed his hands deep into his jacket pockets, and kicked at a mound of fallen leaves. He had conkers in his pocket, and he pulled one out, flipping it from one hand to the other. "I've heard

7

stuff about you – I think my sister's got a picture of you back at our trailer – but I haven't taken much notice. I've got better things to do with my time."

"Sure you have. A place like this must be teeming with excitement."

Nicky flicked the conker into the air. He just missed catching it, and it plopped heavily back amongst the leaves, slipping away beneath the browns and yellows.

Part of him wanted to race away and forget he'd ever been here. But there was one last thing he wanted to know before he went. He might never have been to the cinema, but he suddenly realized that he knew all about the horse. There were posters of her everywhere – and he'd seen her on the telly. The image of her had stuck in his mind. He looked up at Levi again, "So – this must be 'Starlight'? The horse from the last film?"

Levi Buick pulled at a low hanging branch, twisting down a conker still half in its shell. He split the spiky case open and held the conker between his fingers, squinting at it with one eye. "So you're one of the nerds who follow the horse are you?"

"What are you talking about?"

"There's plenty of them. They're all nutcases. Weirdos. They send the horse letters. Cards. Flowers. They want bits of mane. Bits of coat.

Somebody wrote once offering a fortune for bits of shit."

"That's not what I'm doing here." Nicky hated the casual edge to Levi's voice, as if Nicky was some sort of vaguely interesting insect that had crawled across his path. But he still hung on, not quite able to let the moment go. "So – what's she like to ride?"

"This horse is a performance animal. It does what it's trained to do – provided you know what you're doing of course." Levi spun the conker high into the sky, catching it without even looking at it. "And if you knew anything about horses, you'd know that what you just did was really crazy. Stepping out in front of it like that."

Nicky jerked his head up as if Levi had just punched him. "I was going on what I could see."

"I had everything working really well. Kids like you cause us no end of trouble."

Nicky flinched at being called a "kid" – Levi Buick looked older than him, but only by a few years. "Next time I see someone being dragged by a horse I'll look the other way, shall I? So you'd better hope it doesn't just happen to be you."

Levi made a casual, upward movement with his eyebrows. "So if you're not interested in fawning over me or the horse, what exactly are you hanging about for?" He bent to untie the dummy's foot from the stirrup. It slumped to the ground, its strange face still twisted towards Nicky.

Nicky stared down at it. It had glass eyes. Doll's eyes. The sort that open and shut. They were open now, a bright blue. But blank. Empty.

A breeze rippled the branches of the tree, sending a fresh scatter of conkers and leaves to the ground.

Nicky dragged his gaze away from the dummy. "I wasn't hanging about. I've been out looking for work. Me and my dad do land clearance and stuff, and we got a nod that there'd been people over here, measuring up. I'm on my way back from school, but we break up today for half-term. I was seeing if I could line something up to start on Monday..."

"I've heard it all before. We've got signs all over the place to tell people to keep away while we're working, but there's always someone trying to sneak on to the set."

Nicky bristled again. "I came through one of the gardens along the top there – I know someone who lives in one of those houses – so I wouldn't have gone past any of your stupid signs." Nicky didn't add that, even if he had, he wouldn't have been able to read them. His family were Gypsies. They'd spent a lot of time travelling around. For a long time he and Sabrina only used to go to school in the winter. It was horses Nicky had spent his travelling years learning about, not squiggles on paper.

It was different now of course – now they'd had to settle in one place – but there were some things it was too late to catch up on.

Levi gave Nicky a slow, hard look, then skimmed the conker away. It flew long and high, a small red dot spinning off into the distance.

Across at Chestnut Court someone in a midnight-blue cardigan broke away from the cluster by the hedge and ran down the stone steps towards them.

Nicky turned to Starlight. If he was about to be moved on, he could at least get a look at the horse before he went.

His quick eye could see that Starlight was well-bred, and well-cared for.

Her coat shone, and her mane and tail were silky-bright. But it was her face that really caught the beauty of her. It was fine-boned and delicate, the pale gold set off by a streak of white that ran from between her eyes down to her nose. Nicky reached up to touch her, and as his fingers brushed her forehead he felt a spark fizz through him. It was only fleeting, but for a moment it left him buzzing, as if a race of energy had whipped into him.

"Leave it." The turquoise eyes flicked over Nicky. "This animal's insured for millions. We both are."

Nicky let his hand drop back to his side, his fingertips still tingling with Starlight's touch. "I wouldn't hurt her."

"This is a class horse. It needs proper handling. People who know what they're doing. People who know what horses need."

"I –" Nicky glared at Levi. He wanted, more than anything in the whole world, to punch Levi Buick on his multi-million-dollar nose.

"What's going on?" The wearer of the blue cardigan appeared beside them. She was a skinny girl. Nicky guessed she was in her late teens – early twenties at the most. But her dark eyes were older. Restless. Someone who was hungry for something.

She ran an anxious hand through her short, spiked hair and turned to Levi. "You OK?"

"Hi Courtney. Sure – I'm fine. Just the usual stuff." Levi winked at her and gave her a boyish, lop-sided smile. She flushed and smiled back, her thin worried face lighting up suddenly.

Then Levi turned, vaulted up into the saddle, and nudged Starlight forward.

Starlight bucked twice, but Nicky could see Levi was telling her to, keeping her head twisted sideways, then driving her forward with a sharp jab with his left heel.

"Careful." Courtney's voice was tense again. "I'll lose my job if I don't keep you in one piece."

Levi laughed, "If I end up like Humpty Dumpty I know you'll always be there to put me back together again." He kept Starlight prancing as he spoke, her neck arched, her body fluid and beautiful. Then Levi flicked another wink at Courtney and cantered away. He didn't even glance at Nicky.

"You shouldn't be here. You might have ruined the training." Courtney began twisting a sparkling crystal ring round and round her middle finger.

"But I didn't..."

"You should go." Courtney stooped and picked up the dummy, its head squashed under her arm. "If Richard King – the director – comes over he'll be really mad at you. We're on a tight schedule here. We can't afford distractions."

"But I haven't..."

Courtney turned, running after Levi and Starlight as they thundered away towards Chestnut Court.

The woman in the purple dress appeared at the bottom of the steps. She stood very still, staring across at Nicky. She was closer now, and he could see the shadowy shapes around her more clearly. It was three cats – lilac-grey – slinking and pressing against her. Nicky looked away, suddenly scared that she might come over and have a go at him as well.

He glanced back to where Courtney was still

following Levi. As she ran the dummy's legs danced strangely through the swaying grass. Its head was twisted slightly. Even when it was halfway across the field, Nicky could see its blank empty eyes blinking back at him with each bounce and bump.

Nicky shivered. There were clouds blocking the sun now, throwing shadows across the field. The wind was fiercer too, the falling leaves swirling in sudden gusts.

Levi and Starlight reached the steps, and Starlight trotted up them easily. Nicky saw Levi spring off her, then lead her away behind the hedge. Watching her go Nicky felt a pang of longing. She was special. Almost dizzying. He shook the feeling away. She was light-years beyond him. There wasn't any point dreaming about a star he could never reach. And the whole thing with Levi Buick had got to him. He felt as if Levi had scored some sort of point in a game Nicky hadn't even known they were playing.

Pushing his hands deep into his pockets he set off back across the field, taking a sharp left turn that led him away from Chestnut Court and out on to the road.

3

The car slowed down, pulling up on to the verge behind Nicky. It beeped its horn.

Nicky turned to see Maddy Proctor flashing her lights and waving at him. Her car was hitched to a rickety-looking horsebox.

"Hey – Nicky!" Bretta Miles – Nicky's best friend from school – wound down the window on the passenger side. "We were just coming to look for you."

"What's up?" Nicky walked back to them, glad of something to blank out the last half hour. "There's nothing wrong with Sapphire is there? You haven't got trouble with his new owner?"

"The new owner's fine." Maddy leaned out of the window towards him, while a walnut-brown puppy scrambled up from the back seat and sat on her shoulder. "You know it took me ages to choose the right person. And she's only fostered him. If anything goes wrong, he'll come straight back to me."

"So what is it then?" Nicky could tell from the angry blaze in Maddy's eyes, and the way Bretta was twisting her hair round her fingers, that they hadn't been planning to invite him to come back and watch a video.

"Can you hold Russet a minute?" Maddy passed the puppy to Bretta, then turned back to Nicky. "I got a phone call earlier. Someone anonymous — telling me about a donkey that's living in a hell-hole. I only used to get told about dogs being ill-treated, but I've been rung up about all sorts since word got out about Sapphire. I borrowed this horsebox from a friend, and we're going over there now." She rubbed her hand across her forehead, pushing back her ginger bush of hair that was streaked with grey. "We wanted you with us. You'll know how to deal with it better than us."

Nicky hesitated. He'd already been out longer than he should have. Dad would be expecting him back at the site. "What's wrong with this donkey?"

"Apparently it's been kept in someone's garden shed. They never let it out."

"It sounds really awful," added Bretta, her

cornflower-blue eyes dark with worry. "It hasn't been handled for months, so it's gone loopy. Apparently the owner is too scared to go near it, so they've just shut it away. The woman who rang Maddy found out because her little girl saw it through the shed window. She'd gone round to play in the garden."

Nicky closed his eyes for a moment, trying to imagine what that was like to be shut up in a small dark shed for months and months. It would be worse than hell. Nicky couldn't stand being shut up anywhere for five minutes.

He climbed into the back seat. Russet jumped on him immediately and began chewing his left ear. Nicky prised her away, rolling her upside down on his lap and rubbing her tummy gently, "I can't be out long," he said. "But I'll do what I can."

4

The donkey stood, hunched and starving, amongst droppings and old grass-cuttings. Mildew darkened the shed windows with a slimy green film. There was the stench of things rotting.

Nicky waited in the darkness, wedged between a rusting birdcage and a broken rabbit-hutch. On top of the hutch was a pile of old curtains and Nicky pushed them into the space he was crouched in, leaning against them to get comfortable. He didn't try to touch the donkey. He needed to give him time. He needed to let him get a sense of his shape and smell.

Slowly Nicky's eyes got used to the gloom, and he began to get a better look at the donkey. His coat was matted. There were scabs and scars across his face and neck. Nicky heard a rasp in his throat as he breathed.

Nicky closed his eyes, hoping he might pick up something of what the donkey was feeling. He'd done it a lot with horses – sensing moods and fears, seeing colours that marked out hidden damage, or pain. But with this little donkey there was nothing. He was locked deep inside himself. Nicky guessed that was the only place he felt safe.

Outside, he heard voices.

"We bought him as a pet for our little girl, but he's so vicious, he frightens her. None of us can get near him."

"So why didn't you find him a new home straight away – as soon as you knew you couldn't handle him?"

"We didn't want to upset Annabelle. She just wanted to comb him and hug him and tie ribbons in his mane. But he was such a naughty donkey. He wouldn't stand still long enough. He made her nervous. She started to have bad dreams. Nightmares where he kept chasing after her with his funny ears and big teeth. She's such a sweet, sensitive child. She's indoors crying now. Even though he's been upsetting her so much, she still doesn't want him to go."

Nicky heard Maddy give an angry snort.

He tried to tune them both out, just to think

about the donkey. "It's OK mate. You'll be OK. We're going to get you away from here." He kept his tone soft, talking all the time.

The donkey shifted slightly, one ear slanted towards Nicky. At least he was listening.

Nicky straightened up slowly. A tangle of ivy that had wound its way down through a hole in the roof brushed against his hair.

There was a scatter of empty snails' shells on the window-ledge.

A moth hung, fluttering feebly, caught in a spider's web.

Bretta tapped on the shed door and pushed it open. "We have to go soon. The woman's getting funny. I think Maddy's worried she might change her mind."

"Give me a bit longer," Nicky whispered. "I need more time."

Bretta shut the door again.

Nicky moved nearer to the donkey.

The donkey jerked away, his head up, his body suddenly tight and tense.

Nicky stopped again. Left to himself he would have given the donkey as much time as he needed. Left to himself he would have let the donkey come to him.

Nicky took another step nearer, and reached out his hand.

It was the softest of touches, like the brushing of wings against silk, but the donkey shuddered and jumped. Nicky kept his hand steady, feeling the donkey relax again. Leaning into him. It was beginning to work. Nicky was never quite sure exactly what it was he did, but he always sensed the moment when it happened. A moment of magic when a new energy started to flow.

Normally it was a great feeling. Like he'd reached the stars. But this time he felt bad. This little donkey was just going to start to trust him, and he'd have to scare him half to death again. He'd have to drag him out of the shed, and put him through a hellish journey back to Maddy's place.

The donkey had lived in this damp, black hole for months. The late afternoon light would blaze into his eyes. Forgotten sounds and smells would smash against his senses.

Nicky slid his hand along the donkey's neck, his fingers circling gently. He wished he had longer.

"Nicky..." It was Bretta again.

"OK. Leave the door open." Very slowly Nicky lifted one of the curtains. It was raggy and damp, grey mould smothering the pattern of fluffy white kittens chasing butterflies. Nicky wrapped it round the donkey's head. "Stand back. We're coming out."

But there was no need for anyone to stand back. Muffled in the safe familiar smell of the curtain, the donkey let Nicky lead him by the mane out into the garden. Then he stumbled, swaying, following Nicky up the ramp into the horsebox.

5

"**N**o way." Dad's dark hair was specked with sawdust after a day's work chopping logs. "You're not going off to hang around Maddy Proctor's for every spare second again."

Nicky rummaged in his pencil-case for a compass. He was supposed to be drawing and labelling the planets for homework. He had all week, but he wanted to get it over with, so he had a clear space away from anything to do with school for the whole of half-term. "But Maddy *needs* me. She's rescued this donkey and..."

"*I* need you," Dad's voice was a growl. "For one thing I've got trouble with the pick-up. We're going to have to do some major repairs to it if it's going to get us through the winter. Jim's arthritis is really giving him grief, and I can't ask him to untighten bolts and stuff. And on top of that I've got a bloke who wants a load of logging work done, starting first thing Monday morning. I'm relying on you to be there."

Nicky emptied the pencil-case on to the table with a clatter. Jim was Dad's older cousin. He and Nicky slept together in the second trailer. It was good that he was with them, but there would come a time when Jim would find it too hard to help Dad with the tree-felling and land clearance that usually earned them their living. Nicky knew Dad was already thinking about that time – building him up to take Jim's place. Except it wasn't what Nicky wanted. It was horses he lived for. Horses he dreamed about. Dad would never let him actually *have* a horse, but it cut deep with Nicky that he wasn't even allowed to work with them. He tried again. "Why can't I do both? I'll chop logs and stuff with you and Jim through the day, and help Maddy in the evening."

"Evenings are closing in now, and I don't want you gadding about, getting into all sorts of trouble. Your bike's not safe to ride since those gorgio boys twisted the handlebars for you, and I don't want you walking about in the dark." Dad went to the tiny kitchen area where Mum was cleaning the cooker. It was playing up, and a bloke Dad knew was supposed to be coming over to try and fix it.

Dad came back with a can of beer from the fridge.

"I'll only be at Maddy's." Nicky had given up looking for the compass, and pulled out half a dozen conkers from his pockets instead. He put them in a row, rolling them round with his finger for a moment. He didn't collect them for any reason. He just liked them. They reminded him of other times – gathering armfuls with his cousins when they'd lived with the other Gypsies at Beech Common. There'd been swaps and deals. Competitions. Championships. But that was before Dad and Grandad had a fight to end all fights, and Dad had dragged them away from the old life, trying to start up something new.

Nicky chose the biggest conker and drew round it, trying to remember whether it should be Mercury or Mars. He tried to recite in his head the phrase Miss Ekins had made the class say, to help them learn the order of the planets. *My something something something planets...* Nicky couldn't pull the words out of his memory, but it probably didn't matter much. He was as bad at writing as he was at reading. He wouldn't be able to spell them anyway.

He spun the conker in the air, already forgetting about the homework. The only thing that orbited his mind was the thought of the little grey donkey stumbling his way into Maddy's stable, then huddling in the corner. "Please Dad."

"I said no." Dad slumped on the seat next to Nicky and flicked the remote on the telly.

Nicky pulled his thoughts back to what he was supposed to be doing, and chose a conker to draw round for Saturn.

The news came on – a famous actress getting in a deep-purple limousine with three lilac-grey cats on leads. Nicky paused for a moment, recognizing the woman at Chestnut Court, but the story changed to something about homeless teenagers. Nicky didn't want to have to hear about kids forced to live in cardboard boxes. He went back to drawing round conkers again. "Maddy Proctor can't afford to use a vet, and if you *saw* this donkey..."

"Maddy Proctor had no business getting herself an animal that she couldn't pay the bills for. Why should she expect *you* to go over there for nothing? What about your school mate, Bretta? Why doesn't Maddy Proctor ask her?"

"Bretta will lend a hand, but she's got that other horse – Eclipse – to look after." Nicky held up his "Pluto" conker. He liked it because it was small, and an odd shape. It was pointless arguing with Dad once he got into a mood like this anyway. It was pointless trying to tell him that not even Bretta – as brilliant as she was with horses – could straighten the donkey out the way he could. And he knew it wasn't just his spending time with Maddy Proctor that was getting to Dad. His dad's problems with horses went way, way back – right to when he was a kid and he'd seen his sister trampled by a mad horse. Grandad always said Dad never got over losing his sister, and that it changed him. He went deep inside himself, and never properly came back out. But it was a taboo subject. No one was supposed to talk about it.

Nicky had run out of different-sized conkers. His planets looked stupid anyway. Wobbly and pathetic. He should have gone and got some stuff from the tool kit. The ends of hammers, or Jim's socket set, would have done a better job. He picked up his rubber.

At that moment the trailer door swung open, and Sabrina and her best friend Jade burst in. "We've got a ticket. We're going to see *him*."

"See who?" Mum walked in, wiping her hands on a tea-towel.

Sabrina and Jade were almost bouncing. "They're giving out tickets in the newsagents. You ought to get one, Nicky, before they all go."

"Tickets for what?"

"To see Levi Buick. You know they're filming over at Chestnut Court – it's for a new film called *The Other Side of Heaven*. Well, they've invited local children to go over there tomorrow morning... Levi Buick — my *dream* actor." Sabrina was breathless, the words tumbling out, her eyes like stars.

"Oh, I can't believe it. I feel all shivery, just knowing he's nearby." Jade hugged herself, her normally pale cheeks pink with excitement. "Apparently they got fed up with kids hiding in the bushes and things, so they're having an official autograph signing on Saturday."

Nicky felt a hot flush stain his face and his neck. He rubbed harder.

Dad turned down the news as his mobile began to beep, then pulled a face as it went dead as soon as he answered it. "Damn thing's done that twice today."

Nicky glanced up at him. "Perhaps it's because you haven't paid the bill yet, like last month."

Dad scowled at Nicky and pushed the phone roughly back into his pocket. He turned back to Sabrina. "You're not going hanging around a film set on your own. You get all sorts of cranks at places like that."

"Oh Dad..." The spark faded from Sabrina's dark eyes, and she twisted her long brown hair round her fingers, bringing it up to her cheek. "You've got to let me."

"I think it's quite safe, Mr Ghiselli," Jade cut in. "There'll be loads of other kids there, and it's a chance in a million. Levi Buick was in the paper last week. They were giving away free badges and stuff. I gave Sabrina the poster because I've already got loads. He's really..."

"You can only go if Nicky takes you." Dad took another swig of beer.

Nicky looked up so sharply that his hand slipped as he rubbed, pulling a tear in the paper. He wouldn't tell them that he'd met Levi Buick. They'd pounce on him like a couple of kittens with a ball of wool. But he wasn't about to go anywhere that might mean he had to see that jerk again. "What do I want to go for? I don't want his bloody autograph."

"Don't talk like that." Mum came through with cans of coke for Sabrina and Jade. "Dad's right. They'll be safer if you're with them."

"Oh *please* Nicky." Sabrina clasped her hands together like a nun praying in church.

"Yes. *Please*. We'll do anything for you," added Jade.

"Sounds interesting," Nicky said gruffly, rolling the homework into a ball and flinging it towards the bin. "What did you have in mind?"

Jade grinned. "I could do that homework for you, for a start."

"What – the writing and everything?"

"Sure."

"Miss Ekins would know it wasn't mine."

"I won't do it the way I normally write."

Nicky flushed again. "You mean you'll make lots of mistakes?"

Jade looked away. "I didn't mean it to sound like that," she said gently.

Nicky gave her a sharp glance, then shrugged. "I suppose you'll have to do a few spellings and things wrong. You've got to do the planets as well, and get them in the right order."

"That's easy. I learnt that at my last school." Jade began counting them off on her fingers. "Mercury. Venus. Earth. Mars. Jupiter. Saturn. Uranus. Neptune. Pluto. *My Very Easy Method Just Speeds Up Naming Planets.*"

Nicky handed Jade a fresh sheet of paper.

"Thanks Nicky, you're a star." Sabrina hugged him, and then Dad, her eyes sparkling again.

Nicky nodded, then got up and walked outside. He stopped briefly to pat Sky, their Alsatian dog, who was asleep under the trailer. Then he walked on across the site to the muddle of rubbish that was dumped amongst the nettles on the far side, under the trees. A lot of it was stuff Dad and Jim had left there. Nicky hated it that they always had to have rubble around like that, but it cost money to get rid of it at the industrial tips, and things were tight at the moment. There was a pile of old roof-tiles, and

Nicky began picking them up and dropping them into the bottom of a rusted-up supermarket trolley. He worked quickly, pulling up two or three at a time. They made a great sound – a sharp crack and smack – when he dropped them hard enough to smash.

He wouldn't let himself think about anything. Not Dad, or Levi Buick, or the silky-gold horse that had fizzed like a sparkler when he touched her that afternoon. He even pushed away the picture of the thin little donkey in Maddy's stable. He kept his mind empty, his hands growing rough from the edges of the tiles, and his back aching from the endless stooping and bending.

At last the trolley was full.

Nicky leaned back against it, tilting his head and watching the sky. It was a clear night, a cold glitter of stars peppering the black. Miss Ekins had told them you could see about three thousand stars with the naked eye. He wondered how anybody knew that? Who had been crazy enough to count? He screwed up his eyes, trying to capture all that dazzling brightness – a chaos of silver lights rushing and swirling in a million sparkling explosions. And then the image of the donkey crept back into his thoughts, and the star-bright vision shrivelled and died.

Nicky pushed at the trolley with his foot. It

rattled forward, then fell sideways slowly. The tiles spilled out again with a tired clatter.

Nicky stared at them for a moment, then looked back up at the sky again, wondering what the hell was so special about getting some stupid film-star's name on a piece of paper.

6

The queue stretched all along the overgrown drive that curved up through the rusted gates of Chestnut Court. It wound down the lane that ran level with the front of the building. It spilled out into the main road.

It was raining, but nobody seemed to mind.

Nobody except Nicky.

He squelched through the slippy mud to the gate, trying to get a glimpse of what was happening up ahead. The line of soggy, bedraggled children led to a bus. It was no ordinary bus. It glowed midnight-blue, with huge silver stars sprayed across it. The back was painted with a giant Levi Buick, his turquoise eyes and easy smile dazzling and unreal. The windows were tinted, so it was impossible to see inside. Nicky recognized Courtney, huddled under a giant umbrella, standing at the bottom of the steps. She was letting children through slowly, in twos and threes.

Nicky squelched back again to Sabrina and Jade. "I notice Levi's not having to stand in the rain."

"He can't get wet," Sabrina was shivering, dressed in a skimpy top and skirt patterned with sequins and stars. It was supposed to be her best outfit, and Mum didn't know she was wearing it. The carrier bag on her arm held the jeans and sweatshirt that Mum had seen her leave in. Sabrina hugged herself to keep warm. "He might catch a cold. You can't be the star of a film if you've got a runny nose."

"Levi would *never* have a runny nose." Jade wiped at the raindrops that were trickling down from her fringe, and shivered too. Her short black velvet dress was soaked through, and clinging to her. She'd stuffed her "sensible" clothes in the bag with Sabrina's things.

"I bet Levi never farts either," Nicky muttered.

The two girls glared at him, and they all shuffled up a few steps as the queue nudged forwards.

The rain fell harder, drumming tiny craters into the pitted ground.

Two older girls came by, both of them keeping together underneath a silver umbrella. In spite of the rain they looked beautiful.

Sabrina clutched Jade's arm, "Ask them if they're famous."

The first girl, who had a suntan that made her look as if she'd just stepped off the beach in California, heard her and grinned. "My name's Rachel. I work in Make-up. My sister Libby does the costumes. We've come to give out leaflets."

"The director's looking for extras." Libby flicked back a tumble of wild fair hair done all over in tiny plaits, and grinned too. "They're shooting a fireworks scene on Friday night and they need a bit of a crowd – just to stand around and say 'oooh' and 'aaaah' and things like that. If you're interested you just have to fill in the form at the bottom."

Rachel handed out yellow leaflets to Sabrina and Jade. They took them as if she was handing out thousand-pound notes. Libby ducked out from the umbrella and tried to give one to Nicky, but he shook his head and pushed his hands deep into his pockets.

She smiled, shrugged, then hurried to catch up with her sister who was moving on down the line.

A man came by, handing out hot dogs. "Keep your strength up, my sweethearts." He winked at Jade and Sabrina. "We don't want you fainting before the big moment."

Sabrina took a bite from her hot dog and sparkled

up at him. "We'll probably faint as soon as we see him anyway."

The man winked again, "Well, perhaps he'll give you the kiss of life."

Sabrina and Jade giggled and squealed.

The man moved on.

Sabrina nudged Jade, her teeth chattering with cold. "Everyone here's so nice. I'm having a brilliant time."

"Me too." Jade wiped a smudge of tomato sauce off her lips, and tried to wring the bottom of her dress with the other hand. The water poured out solidly, like a tap running. When she'd finished, the dress looked different – pulled into a funny shape down one side.

Nicky bit into his hot dog. The roll was already soggy. The queue hadn't moved for five minutes. "Look, I'm bored with this, and there's no way I want to see this Levi bloke. I'm going to look around a bit. There's a few big trailers and things about – I think it's OK to look inside them, and I want to kill a bit of time."

"How can you bear not to see Levi?" Sabrina pulled a face at him. "You'll be sorry later."

"I'll get over it." Nicky spun the remains of his hot dog into a nearby bin. "I'll be back in half an hour. You might have made it as far as the gate by then."

He grinned at them both, walked along the edge of the queue, and into the grounds of Chestnut Court.

There were huge trailers everywhere. A couple of caravans. A massive marquee.

And it was busy. Film crew battled against the rain, appearing and disappearing between the trailers and caravans.

An enormous man with a shock of red hair paced the length of the terrace, stopping every now and then to growl something at a huddle of people clustered round a television monitor. A short stocky man stood on the top of some stone steps that led down to the grounds, scanning the rain-misted view with a camera.

Nicky noticed another trailer – deep purple and black, the sort of super-deluxe type Mum always dreamed of having – and he wandered towards it. It was set back from the others, outside the hub of everything. He walked all round it, wondering what it was like inside. Suddenly he caught a movement at the window. A woman's face appeared fleetingly, then ducked away again.

Nick turned away, flushing as he remembered the time a bunch of gorgios had driven slowly past their trailers, taking pictures of his family as if they were monkeys in a zoo. Now he was doing the same sort of thing.

Arrows were pointing towards three more trailers – not homes this time, but huge container types. Two of them were locked, but the third one had signs tied to the outside that even Nicky could manage. PROPS and OPEN.

Nicky walked up the steps.

A girl – fluffy fair hair and marshmallow-soft skin – got up from a strawberry-pink armchair to greet him. "Hi. I'm Suzy. I'm a drama student, doing a couple of weeks on location." She put down the notebook she was scribbling into and offered him a toffee. "They've stuck me in here for the morning. I'm s'posed to be interesting and entertaining for anyone that comes in. What shall I tell you?"

Nicky shrugged. "I'm just hanging around really, waiting for my sister and her mate."

Suzy gave him a sugary smile, twisting a sparkling crystal ring round her plump middle finger. "So have you got Levi's autograph already?"

"I don't want it."

The powder-blue eyes darkened in disbelief. "Do you know much about the new film?"

Nicky wiped his dripping forehead with the back of his hand and shook his head. He wasn't going to admit that he'd never been to the cinema in his life before. Nicky hated closed-in places – places he couldn't just come and go from. He'd rather stand all day in the rain than sit for two hours in a darkened room where he might not be able to see the door. "I've been too busy," he said at last.

Suzy's smile sweetened again, "You do know we've got Elinora Moon co-starring alongside Levi don't you?"

"Sure." Nicky looked away, hoping she wasn't going to ask him any questions that might catch him out.

"I studied her at college." Suzy's voice was honey soft. "She's great. She can play any part. Be anything she wants. She's a bit unusual, but she's amazing to watch, don't you think?"

"Amazing."

"And those cats. They go with her everywhere. She's got a real gift with them – it's like they've got this magic bond between them. It's brilliant, isn't it?"

"Brilliant."

"You know, she can't see very well, so they have to put all her scripts on to tape. She just learns them by listening. I found that out when I was doing my thesis on her. It's fantastic, isn't it?"

"Fantastic."

"But she's got such wonderful eyes when you get up close to her. Deep green and mysterious. She's just right for the Gypsy woman in *The Other Side of Heaven*."

"Gypsy woman?" Nicky felt a spark of interest. "So what's that bit about?"

"She's got this kind of passion for the character Levi plays – it's like an obsession – and she starts following him around. Only he doesn't really take any notice of her. He just thinks she's a kind of nutcase. That's until she starts to use her Gypsy powers..."

Nicky gave her a long look. He should have guessed any gorgio story with a Gypsy in it would have to be loaded with dark troubles and curses. "So what does she do?"

"Well, I'm not supposed to tell you the story. Richard King – that's the director – says its bad luck, and we don't want to give any secrets away. But I s'pose a bit won't hurt. I mean, just through the advertising everyone's going to know that she..."

Suddenly the door burst open, a gust of rain blasting in. Three girls appeared. They were all wet through, and crying.

Suzy's eyes grew rounder than gobstoppers. "What's happened? Is somebody hurt?"

"We saw him," moaned the tallest girl, clutching her autograph book to her chest. "We *saw* him."

"He smiled at me," sobbed the second one. "And he was so beautiful. Like a golden angel who'd just drifted down from the clouds. And he asked me my name."

The third girl just hugged herself tightly, and groaned.

Nicky looked at them all. Suzy was fussing round them. She glanced up at Nicky just once, as if she was surprised to discover he was still there. "Have a walk through, and ask me any questions at the end. Just don't touch anything, and don't drip on anything. I'll get swallowed whole if anything gets damaged. It would be a disaster for the continuity of the film. We'd have to go through all those shots again." She hugged the girls harder. The first two had stopped crying now, and were showing her their autograph books. Suzy settled the third girl in the strawberry-pink armchair. There was a pile of fabric draped over the back of the chair. Suzy rummaged amongst it, pulling up a creamy-yellow curtain, and folding it round the girl.

Nicky wandered deeper into the trailer. It was crammed tight with furniture and ornaments; plastic food; flower-tubs; a plaster statue. He hated the muddle. The way it all hemmed him in. It was only the rattle of rain on the metal roof that kept him in there.

There were labels stuck to everything. Nicky didn't have a clue what any of them said, so he walked on towards the back of the trailer.

Then suddenly he saw them.

Hanging upside down in rows, their feet hooked to a metal rail.

Dummies. All with the floppy sun-blond hair. The Levi Buick check shirt and jeans. The blank empty eyes.

"Hey – look at these." The two girls appeared behind him. They had stopped crying – they were just sniffing, and chewing toffees loudly.

"They're weird."

"They're gross."

"Why are there so many?"

"These are the new ones. We've got a mountain of used ones in the cellar that runs under Chestnut Court. They're only made of foam and wire, so they get damaged easily." Suzy came over and took one down from the rail. She turned it the right way up, fussing with its shirt and running her fingers through its hair. "We do lots of takes. Different angles. Different lights. These little sweethearts get dragged by Starlight, so we can only use each one once. It can take us around eight hours to shoot four or five minutes of screen time, and..."

"Starlight!" The tallest girl gave a tiny shriek, and burst into tears again.

Nicky suddenly didn't want to be in here any more. He wanted to be somewhere with space around him. Somewhere sane. Somewhere alone.

He turned quickly, hurrying past the creamy-yellow curtain that was still sobbing softly in the chair.

He took a deep breath as he got outside. Standing in the swirling wind and rain suddenly seemed like a treat.

7

"Maddy's decided to call him Dusty." Bretta walked towards Nicky as he came round the outside of the stable.

Russet bounded out from round the opposite corner and piddled with excitement.

Nicky leaned against the stable door. Dusty was standing with his back to him, hunched and huddled against the partition in the middle of the stall. It was almost exactly the same position he had been in when he was in the shed. "Has Maddy done much with him?"

"Neither of us have been able to get close. Maddy got the vet to come, but even she had trouble this morning. She cleaned up his cuts and sorted out his hooves. But she said – she said it might be kinder if..." Bretta's voice trailed away, then she looked at Nicky. "I was hoping you'd come over, but I wasn't sure if your Dad would let you."

"He hasn't," Nicky slid the bolt on the stable door. "Not officially anyway. But I reckoned I earned it. I had to take Sabrina and Jade to see that Levi Buick bloke this morning. We had to queue up for ages."

Bretta pulled a face. "In all that rain?"

"In all that rain."

"They must be nuts."

Nicky grinned at her suddenly. Bretta always managed to make him feel better.

He was about to close the stable door again when Russet bounced in. She sat down suddenly, her soft, round body pressed up against Dusty's back leg.

"I'll take her out..." Bretta bent to pick her up but Nicky shook his head.

"Leave her. Dusty's not bothered at the moment, and you never know what works with animals."

"I'll go then," said Bretta. "Come and find me when you've finished."

"Hang on –" Nicky called her back suddenly. "You can stay if you want."

Bretta's eyes held his. "Are you sure?"

Nicky shifted awkwardly, not sure suddenly why he'd said it. "You – you won't laugh?"

"What about?"

"Well – the way I work. The things I do."

Bretta's voice was very soft. "I would love to be able to do even a quarter of what you do. You letting me stay makes me feel really..." she hesitated, as if it was her who was feeling awkward now, "well, proud I s'pose. But if you're not really happy about it..."

A silence hung between them.

Then Nicky straightened up and looked at her. "No. I'm sure. I might get hit on the head by a stray meteorite tomorrow. I won't have helped Dusty at all if no one else can handle him." He gave Bretta a quick smile. He had never really done anything like this before – not shared the Gypsy secrets he'd learned from Grandad – but Bretta was his best mate. She was one of the few gorgios he could trust.

Bretta smiled back. "Thanks. I know what it means to you. And I won't tell anyone else – it'll just be something between me and you."

Nicky nodded, suddenly impatient to get on with the job.

As he reached his hand up towards Dusty he felt a rush of energy. He was excited about Bretta being there. It was as if he was standing on the edge of something new.

Nicky didn't touch the donkey. Instead, he held his hands out over the thin grey body, as if he was warming himself against a flame. "It's important not to move too soon. I do as little as I can. I'm trying to let him have a feeling of control."

"What do you mean?" Bretta was whispering.

"I suppose..." Nicky spoke slowly, sorting out exactly what he wanted Bretta to know. If he was going to pass this stuff on, he had to explain it right. "I suppose I mean that this shouldn't be me coming to him. It should be him coming to me. And if it seems he's not handling it, then I'll stop until he's ready again."

"How will you know?"

Nicky stepped nearer, moving his hands, following the shape of Dusty's body. "I just start to feel things. I sort of get drawn towards the bits that matter."

"Are you being drawn now?"

"Everything's blocked. Heavy. He doesn't want to let me in." Very slowly, the touch of his fingers softer than the wings of a moth, Nicky let his hands settle upon the thin, grey back.

Dusty snorted suddenly, and trembled.

Nicky pressed deeper, his hands moving in slow circles.

Bretta leaned forward. "I feel like I should be taking notes."

"There's not a rule. It's different with each animal. That's why you have to spend a bit of time at the beginning, trying to get the feel of what's wrong."

47

"I'd be scared. I'd worry about messing it up."

Nicky thought for a moment. He'd never messed up before. What he did just seemed to work. But it wasn't magic or anything. It was just to do with listening to the invisible signals. "I think as long as you really want it to work, then it will."

He fell quiet, stroking gently, moving his hands along the donkey's legs and back, then sliding his fingers up to the mane. The colours were coming now, muted and soft. At last Dusty was letting him in.

Outside the wind gusted, sighing through the branches of all the trees.

Russet whimpered, chasing imaginary leaves in her sleep.

Bretta hugged her arms tight to her chest, her eyes never leaving Nicky's hands.

Nicky reached the donkey's ears. He pulled at each one gently, supporting Dusty's head with his other hand. Then he reached down on to the soft grey forehead, pressing hard at the spot between his eyes.

Dusty pushed his nose deep into Nicky's chest. Then suddenly he stretched all four legs, raised up his neck, and brayed.

Nicky laughed.

Russet woke up with a yelp.

Bretta burst into tears.

"I reckon we've pressed the right buttons." Nicky grinned. "I'll come over first thing tomorrow morning, before I go off knocking on doors trying to pull in a bit of extra gardening work for next week. Meet me here, and I'll see if I can persuade Dusty to step outside and discover the big wide world."

8

It was a beautiful morning, the sky electric blue, the trees blazing with golds and yellows.

Nicky left the stable door open, letting it swing wide, and stepped outside.

He stood just beyond the door, keeping very still.

He didn't even look round as Bretta rode up on Eclipse, tethered her to a post at the far end of Maddy's garden, then walked over to join him.

Nicky felt something pulling at his feet. Russet had bounced out and was beginning to play tug of war with the laces on his trainers.

Nicky still didn't move. He didn't even look down.

There was a sound behind him. The soft tread of unshod hooves. A gentle breath down the back of his neck. Dusty was out.

Nicky took two steps forward. Russet yelped with excitement at this new game, then bounced back to attack the lace on the other trainer.

Dusty followed.

Nicky took four steps.

Russet slid along behind, her teeth locked on to Nicky's heel.

Dusty followed.

Nicky walked to the tiny gate at the back of the garden – the one that led out on to the field between Maddy's garden and Chestnut Court – and stopped.

Russet fell over.

Dusty pressed his nose into Nicky's shoulder, and brayed softly.

With a quick grin at Bretta, Nicky pushed open the gate and led his strange party out into the field.

9

There was a trampled path round the edge by the fence. The field was roped off halfway across.

"Are you sure it's OK for us to be here?" Bretta whispered, falling into step beside Nicky. "There's signs up everywhere saying this field's been taken over by that film lot."

"We'll keep to the track, away from those ropes. It's a public footpath. I don't reckon they can stop us. And we won't be in anyone's way." Nicky kept walking, letting Dusty follow.

"I s'pose not." Bretta shrugged, glancing back over her shoulder at Dusty. "He's keeping really close, isn't he? It's like he's glued to you."

"It's what they do in the wild. It's about safety.

For any herd animal, being alone can be a death sentence."

Russet raced and chased, bouncing as if her legs were on springs as she tried to see above the grass.

Beyond the hedge Chestnut Court glittered like a fairy-tale palace. As he drew nearer Nicky could hear voices. Occasional shouting.

Nicky changed direction. Dusty was calm and he wanted to keep it that way.

"We'll make our way back now," Nicky decided. "I reckon he's had enough excitement for one day."

Suddenly, from over near the hedge, there was a shout.

A woman appeared, holding up a clapboard.

Somebody shouted, "Stand by please."

Somebody shouted, "Action!"

And Starlight, with Levi leaning close along her neck, burst into the field.

They were galloping fast. A car – a kind of pick-up truck – was keeping pace with them. Four men with a camera were crouched in the open back.

They kept going, heading towards the chestnut tree.

Then suddenly there was another movement.

Nicky turned, his voice locking in his throat, as a shadowy grey cat seemed to spring from nowhere. It shot across the field, just ahead and to one side of Starlight.

Russet, with a yelp of excitement, raced towards it, hurtling under the rope. The tip of her tail caught the "Keep Off" sign, making it swing backwards with a shudder.

The woman in the purple dress appeared at the bottom of the steps. For a moment she stood rigid, as if she was too shocked to move. Then she gave a strange high call – more bird than human. The cat jumped, an effortless leap into the branches of the tree.

But it was too late to stop Russet.

In what seemed like slow motion, Nicky saw her cut straight across the path of Levi and Starlight.

Starlight twisted in the air, trying to jump clear. But she was too close to the tree, and as she landed she skidded straight into it. A tangle of branches scratched at her face and neck. Levi lay low along her, then seemed to crumple away. His body slipped sideways, throwing up sparks of burnt yellow leaves as Starlight dragged him across the ground under the tree.

10

Bretta was the first one to reach Levi. Nicky saw her stoop, bending over him, then look up frantically for help.

There were plenty of people. Too many people. Nicky could hear someone shouting for them to "Keep back. Keep back."

From the break in the hedge two men ran through with a stretcher.

Nicky could see glimpses of Levi, crumpled like a dummy in the grass. But there was nothing he could do. Nothing that would make any difference.

Russet hurtled back to Nicky, yelping and shivering with her tail between her legs.

Nicky picked her up, pressing her close to his chest, then raced to the far end of the field.

Starlight was standing pressed against the fence, her ears flattened and her eyes wild.

Two men ran ahead of him. Nicky could hear them cursing. One of them – a great hulk of a man with a lion's mane of red hair, turned and growled at Nicky, "Stay out of this."

The other, short and stocky, a camera on one shoulder, dropped back.

Nicky ran on, overtaking the red-haired man and ignoring his shouts. Starlight was lame. She stood sideways on to him, her left foreleg hanging awkwardly at an odd angle. He had to get to her before she knocked herself about any further.

"Christ," Nicky heard the red-haired man arrive, panting, behind him. He turned, seeing him put his hands to his forehead in frustrated despair. Everything about him was huge. Huge head. Huge neck. Thick fingers. Thick thumbs. And his voice, even lowered, was a grumbling roar. "She's broken her leg."

"It's not broken," Nicky said softly. "But it could get worse if she tries to run on it."

The man shot a fierce look at Nicky. "Then we've got to stop her." He lurched forwards, making a lunge for her reins. Starlight stumbled sideways, out of his reach.

"It's no good grabbing at her. We've got to get her calm first."

"So what do you suggest? Shall I sing her a lullaby?"

Nicky could see Starlight trembling. He kept his voice soft. "I'll sort her out."

"I can't afford to let you near her. She's worth a fortune. We've got a film to make. My assistant's rung for the vet..."

Starlight threw her head high, her ears pinned against her neck. She tried to take a step backwards, but stumbled again. The reins were dangling dangerously near her lame leg. If she got snagged up on them Nicky knew she'd really panic.

"You haven't got time for the vet. And you can't afford *not* to let me near her. Trust me." As he spoke, Nicky thrust Russet suddenly into the man's arms. Russet wagged her tail, licked his face and piddled on him. The man stared down at Russet, at the damp patch on his shirt, and back up at Nicky.

Nicky wasn't even looking. His eyes were fixed beyond Starlight, staring past her, letting her know he was no threat.

She kept her ears back and flicked her tail, but she stayed where she was.

Nicky could smell the sweat on her, and the red flecks on her neck and shoulders were not make-up this time. "It's OK. I can sort you out. Just take it easy."

From out on the road he heard the wail of sirens.

Starlight snorted, her ears flattened.

Nicky glanced over his shoulders at the man. "She wants me to help her. She's scared and she's in pain. But she's not taking any chances. She's not quite sure of me yet."

"Maybe if you can get near enough to grab hold of those reins..."

"Maybe I can send her crazy again." Nicky shook his head. "I can't rush it."

There was a high beeping noise. The man's mobile phone was ringing. Nicky blanked out the sound and turned back to Starlight.

He could see where the pain was – a knot in her leg where the muscles had overstretched when she'd twisted earlier. He reached his hand out towards it, whispering soft Gypsy words learnt from his days with Grandad. Nicky was never sure what they meant, but it didn't matter. They kept him calm, and they kept horses calm too.

Starlight's ears were flickering now, and her head dropped. "She's interested," Nicky said. He wasn't sure if the man was listening or not, but he didn't want to risk him mucking things up again. "Lowering her head like that is a kind of message. She'll let me touch her now."

From somewhere behind him, on the other side of the field, the wail from the sirens grew louder, and then stopped.

Starlight stood quietly as Nicky put his hands on her neck. Straight away Nicky felt that jolt, that flash of something coming from her and into him – the way it had been in the field that first day. He wished he had time to think about it, but behind him he heard the man growling instructions into his mobile again, and he had to pull his thoughts round and get on with the job.

He pressed against her, gradually moving down her body. Then, lifting her hoof in both hands, he began to stretch and turn it, just using small movements, first one way and then the other. Then he placed her hoof gently back on the ground. Running one finger lightly along the length of her leg, he circled the knot. For a moment there was a swirl of tension. Starlight stiffened again and Nicky felt a jolt of pain in his left arm. And then it was gone. There was just a lightness, like a stream flowing. Starlight relaxed. Nicky stroked her nose and she nuzzled into him. Her eyes, very dark and soft, watched him with a quiet curiosity.

Across the field the siren started up again. Nicky heard it making its way back along the road and fading away towards the town.

"I'll help you take Starlight in," Nicky said, taking a step backwards. He became aware of the cameraman hovering in the background, and suddenly remembered Levi Buick. He swung round to look where he'd fallen. A small group of people were still there, talking and writing in notebooks. A television van had arrived. People were buzzing around filming and taking photographs of the tree.

There was no sign of Bretta. Nicky thought it was odd that she should just go off without telling him. He decided she must be over at Chestnut Court being interviewed or something.

Nicky suddenly remembered what had caused the accident – Russet chasing that cat. He stopped walking, suddenly uneasy. What if they sued him for messing everything up? He turned to the red-headed man nervously. "What about Levi?"

"His chaperone's gone to the hospital with him. I'm waiting for her to call back."

"Do you think he's OK?"

"He's pretty tough. His parents own a ranch in California. He's ridden all his life – he must have had plenty of falls."

Nicky felt an odd twist of envy, "So – he's grown up with horses then?"

"Born in the saddle. I'm hoping..."

Suddenly there was a sound. A harsh, hard braying from right behind Nicky. He swore softly, swinging back round. He'd forgotten Dusty was still with him. Starlight would erupt again.

But Starlight didn't erupt. Her head tipped slightly, she neighed a soft reply, then walked in a direct line towards the donkey. She pressed her nose into his tail. Dusty's nose was still against Nicky's back.

Nicky turned and walked across the field towards Chestnut Court. Dusty, and then Starlight, followed behind.

Russet gave a sudden whimper, squirmed out of the man's arms and joined on behind Starlight, bouncing excitedly at the end of the line.

"Christ." Nicky heard the growled whisper behind him. "What is this kid? The Pied Piper or something?"

Through the gap in the hedge the dark-blue Land Rover of the Maybridge horse vet bumped its way into the field.

The man grunted something at Nicky and walked towards it, followed by the man with the camera.

Nicky took his chance. There were a couple of blokes in headphones still hanging around, and Nicky handed Starlight to them. "She's OK now," he said quickly. "Just lead her to the vet over there. I expect she'll want to check her over."

He touched Starlight's forehead, feeling that spark flash between them again. Nicky had loved lots of horses, for lots of reasons, but Starlight seemed to pull at him in a way he'd never felt before. But there wasn't any point hanging around her.

He'd just end up looking like one of those freaks Levi had been going on about. He turned quickly, escaping across the field with Dusty and Russet before the lion man decided to ask him his name.

11

"Have you heard about Levi?" Sabrina was kneeling, sobbing, on the trailer floor. A poster of Levi Buick was spread out in front of her.

"What about him?" Nicky got himself a Coke from the fridge, and shot Dad a guarded look. If he told her what he knew, he would have to tell her how he knew it. And Dad thought he'd just been out knocking on doors all day.

"There's been a terrible accident. Jade came round just now. She said Levi's paralysed from the neck down." Sabrina lifted the poster gently and hugged it to her chest.

Nicky sat down next to Dad.

Dad flicked the remote on the telly to change

channels from a programme about cars to the early evening news.

"So what happened?" Nicky snapped open the can and tried to keep his expression blank.

"Jade says someone tried to kidnap him. It was some fan who went mad when Levi couldn't sign her autograph book because he was busy filming. This fan had a gun, and she shot at both Levi and Starlight. They're in a bad way..." Her voice wobbled into nothing.

"How did Jade know all that?"

"Her cousin told her."

"And how did the cousin know?"

"Her cousin's best friend. And this best friend's dad knows the producer – so it must all be true."

Sabrina squeezed her eyes shut, tears running like tiny streams down her cheeks.

Nicky put his Coke on the table and leaned towards her. "Levi's tougher than you think."

Sabrina looked at him as if she was drowning and he was the rope she could make a grab at. "Do you think so?"

"I know so. He grew up on a ranch in California. He's a real cowboy – just like those you see on telly. He's probably used to being shot at."

"How d'you know that?"

Nicky glanced sideways at Dad, then back at Sabrina. "My cousin told me."

Sabrina wiped her eyes with the back of her hand, and frowned. "Our cousins are at Beech Common. When did you...?"

But Sabrina didn't finish the sentence. She clapped her hands over her mouth and squealed. Levi's face was filling the television screen.

"Levi Buick, teenage heart-throb and star of last year's blockbuster film The Darkness *was injured today following an incident at Chestnut Court, in Maybridge. He is currently there on location filming a new production called* The Other Side of Heaven.

Richard King, the director, has issued a statement to say that Levi has suffered cuts and bruises, but there has been no serious injury."

Sabrina gripped Nicky's hand. Nicky could feel her fingernails digging into him but he didn't move. The screen image changed from Levi to Starlight. It gave him a jolt, looking at her on his own telly. She seemed brighter, more beautiful, but more unreachable. She was worlds away from him. As distant as Pluto.

"The horse, Starlight, another major star in her own right, was also injured in the incident. Richard King and a member of the camera crew went to her aid, but

she was in pain and frightened. There were fears that she might do herself more damage before she could be caught.

However, an unknown boy — possibly a local youth — not only calmed the mare but also performed a seemingly miraculous cure on her damaged leg.

We are able to bring you footage of the scene, taken by a member of the film crew at the time."

There were flashes of Chestnut Court. An ambulance. A stretcher. Close-ups of faces. People looking shocked. Courtney crying. Someone running along beside the stretcher, holding Levi's hand. Nicky squinted at the slim, brown-haired figure and then realized with a jolt that it was Bretta.

The scene widened to take in more of the field.

Nicky watched in horror. For one crazy moment he wondered if he should sing a song. Break the telly. Pretend to be horribly ill. But nothing he did would stop this happening. Nothing he did would make any difference.

Mum came through, carrying a spray can of oven cleaner.

Sabrina dropped Nicky's hand and let the Levi Buick poster slide down into her lap.

Nicky saw the shot of himself out in the field, one arm stretched out towards Starlight, and Dusty pressed up close behind him.

Dad stood up so quickly he knocked the table. Nicky's Coke can toppled sideways and rolled, the brown fizz oozing down on to the floor.

Dad didn't notice. He stood so near the telly that it looked like he was going to climb inside.

Nicky couldn't see the screen any more, but from the way Dad's shoulders seemed to rise and spread, there was no need. "I ... I was helping out with Maddy Proctor's donkey. That one I told you about."

Dad turned slowly. "You were meant to be looking for work."

Nicky's excuses fluttered like a moth on a web. "It was early. And Sunday morning. You know that's not a good time. I've been out knocking doors for the rest of the day..."

"You just can't get it, can you? You're not supposed to be hanging about with horses. Not Maddy Proctor's. Not Levi Whats-his-face. Even if the frigging Gypsy King came round and asked you to sort his horse out, I wouldn't let you. Horses bring us trouble – they always have – and we don't need it. Get it?"

Something exploded in Nicky. Things he'd thought about before, but never said, suddenly fizzed up and exploded. "They brought *you* trouble – just once – with your sister. But that's nothing to do with me. And it was just one horse. One crazy horse, and a stupid accident, years and years ago. Do you think families of people who get killed in a car accident never drive cars? Do you think families of people who get electrocuted live in the dark for ever and ever? You're just stuck in the past – it's like a bit of you never grew up..."

There was silence, Dad and Nicky breathing hard as if they'd been throwing punches with fists, not words. Then Dad's fingers closed on Nicky's shoulder, wrenching him off the seat.

Sabrina picked up the Levi Buick poster and slipped away.

"Joe..." Mum got a bowl and a cloth, and knelt down to mop at the spilt Coke. "Go easy on him."

Dad's eyes seemed to drill into Nicky's head. His voice was steel. He gripped Nicky tighter. "You think you can do what you like don't you? I'm sick of this horse rubbish – as if you think you're some kind of bloody magician with them. Do you think if a horse tramples on you your bones won't snap the same as anyone else's?"

Nicky stared at Mum's back as she rubbed at the floor, and didn't answer.

Dad gave Nicky a sudden shove, sending him backwards into the seat. His teeth jarred as if he'd been hit. "That's your half-term sorted out. You work with me and Jim every day, and you come back and do whatever I tell you in the evening. You're not going out of my sight. Get it?"

Mum squeezed the cloth out into the bowl, and carried it silently to the sink.

Nicky locked eyes with Dad, but the cold fury in Dad's eyes scared him. Nicky was first to look away.

Mum came back with a can of beer for Dad. He took it from her silently, then stood gripping it so hard that the side dented in.

Outside the trailer Sky started barking.

There was a knock on the door.

"There's someone here," called Sabrina softly. "He says his name's Richard King. The director of *The Other Side of Heaven*."

Nicky looked up to see the red-headed man framed in the doorway.

12

Richard King filled the trailer. Even Dad seemed small beside him.

Nicky wouldn't look at him. He felt cheated. He'd heard once that native North American Indians never liked their photographs being taken because it stole away their soul. Nicky knew how they felt. Richard King and the bloke with the camera had stolen something from him, handed it round for other people to look at, and just left him with a trail of trouble.

"I take it you've seen the news?" Richard King's eyes were light brown – almost yellow – under thick red eyebrows.

"I didn't know you were filming me."

"That was Dave, the cameraman." Richard King

refused Dad's offer of a beer with a shake of his head. "Cameramen are like that. They never miss an opportunity..."

"I wasn't an opportunity." Nicky looked at him sullenly. "I was sorting your horse out for you. You had no right."

The yellow eyes flicked over Nicky. "Your dog caused us a lot of problems, but I'm prepared to let that go."

"I didn't expect there to be a cat out there."

"The cat belongs to Elinora Moon. It was loose by mistake. She accepts it was partly her fault. If it wasn't for her insisting on that fact, I might have been round here with a solicitor's letter. We did have plenty of signs up telling the public to keep away."

"Russet's a bit young for reading. She hasn't started school yet."

"So —" Dad had almost choked on his beer at the mention of solicitors — "at the door you talked about needing some work doing. We do all sorts — me, Nicky and Jim. Mending stuff. Tree clearance. Bit of woodwork."

"I'm going to talk straight with you. We're in a bit of a fix."

"Go on." Dad wiped a froth of beer from his top lip, and Nicky watched him relax. You could make good money out of gorgios in "a bit of a fix".

"I don't know how much you know about

filming, but we're on a schedule – a really tight schedule."

Mum came in carrying a cup of tea in her best bone china cup.

Richard King took it without looking at her. The pink rosebud pattern looked ridiculous in his huge hands. Nicky had a sudden image that he could crush it, the whole thing smattering into tiny pieces, and not even know what he'd done. "We don't have time for things to go wrong. We're supposed to tie things up here by the end of next week. If we get held up beyond that we'd have to re-shoot a lot of the outdoor scenes. Continuity is vital – with all the leaves falling even the trees are different from one day to the next. If we're not filming, we still have to pay retainers to a lot of the crew, just to keep them with us. The list of expenses goes on and on..."

"So – what would you want us to do?" Dad was turning his beer can slowly round in his hand.

"The vet says we should rest Starlight – just to make sure her leg's OK. But that would mean we couldn't film the crucial scene that we were working on today. And we can't substitute the horse – Starlight is as big a name as Levi Buick. *The Other Side of Heaven* might even flop if we did that. So..." Richard King's eyes were suddenly hungry, fixed on Dad as if Nicky wasn't even there. "I want to get your boy to come over – work with the horse like he did today. Keep her in top form till we move on at the end of the week. We're prepared to pay generously, of course."

"My brother – working with Levi Buick?" Sabrina hugged herself tightly, as if she was trying to hold herself together.

Mum took the teacup from Richard King and stood, one finger tracing the gold-patterned rim, her dark eyes resting on Dad.

Dad's face tightened. He folded his arms across his chest and sat very still.

Nicky turned away. Thoughts whirled through his head like leaves in the wind. He was being asked to work with *Starlight*. A picture of her flashed into his head. That glittering gold body. The dark depths in her eyes. The way she moved. But it wasn't just how she looked that had touched him. He'd seen beautiful horses before. But with her there was something different. Something about her that drew him – as if she was a chest full of secret treasure, and Richard King was holding out the key...

"No." Dad shook his head. "He's not working with a horse."

"You can name your price," Richard King's eyes narrowed to slits of yellow.

"Joe..." said Mum gently. "Don't you think...?"

"Dad, *please*," begged Sabrina.

"I'm open to suggestions," said Richard King.

"I said NO!"

The storm burst suddenly in Nicky. "To hell with you then!" He flashed a look at Dad, his face dark and thunderous. Then he pushed his way out of the trailer and into the dusky evening.

13

Nicky didn't go far.

He sat with Sky, watching the trolley and the brick rubble turn to dark lumps in the thickening night.

Sky whimpered and pressed herself against him. Nicky rubbed her ears, glad of the warmth of her body.

He saw Richard King come outside and climb into his green Land Rover and roar away.

He saw Dad stand watching him go.

And he saw the dream of being with Starlight shatter like a silver explosion, all the tiny glittering possibilities fizzing to nothing, like a burnt-out firework.

14

It was Sabrina who came out to find him. "Are you OK?"

Nicky's hand tightened on Sky's collar. "Why should I care? It's nothing new."

"If someone had asked me to spend a week with Levi Buick, and Dad had said no..."

Nicky turned to look at her in the darkness. "I'm stuck for ever with knocking on gorgios' doors, cutting back gorgios' trees, scratching and scraping for work I don't even want to do."

From inside the trailer Nicky heard raised voices. Dad shouting. Mum shouting. He felt cold inside. Mum hardly ever argued back.

Nicky tipped his head up, staring at the purple night and trying to block out their voices. Miss

Ekins had told them that a lot of the stars they could see from earth weren't really there. They were dead stars – burnt out and turned to dust. What they were seeing was just the light that was travelling from them. It made Nicky feel weird, thinking about it.

From inside the trailer came the sound of china breaking.

Sabrina put her hands over her ears, and Nicky put his arm round her shoulder. What the hell did any of it really matter?

Whether he worked with Starlight, or whether he didn't?

Whether Dad stayed a pain all his life, or whether he didn't.

In a hundred years from now they'd be nothing. Nowhere. Less than dust in space.

From inside the trailer everything went quiet. Nicky wasn't sure if that was good – or bad.

"What are you thinking?" Sabrina nudged him gently.

Nicky shook his head. "You don't want to know."

"Go on. Tell me."

He hesitated. "I was just thinking how interesting the stars are."

Sabrina leaned her head against him. "Does that mean you think everything's going to be all right?"

"It means I've decided it doesn't matter."

"I just wish..." Sabrina stopped suddenly, pointing. "Did you see that – that flash of light? A shooting star."

"Aren't they supposed to be...?" Nicky's answer was broken by the trailer door opening. He heard the soft shush of Mum's footsteps coming towards them through the grass.

She crouched down beside them. "I've been talking to Dad – about how money's really tight and everything at the moment. We've made a sort of agreement."

Nicky scowled. "What – that we all put a coin in a box every time anyone says the word 'horse'?"

"Don't be so hard on your Dad. In some ways you're a lot like him – like he was at your age."

"Oh great. I can't wait to grow up now. I can be grumpy and..."

"Just listen to me." Mum pushed her hair back behind her ears. She looked tired. Even in the darkness Nicky could see that her eyes were shadowed. "Dad says he'll think about it – about you working with that film horse. But only if that director bloke gives us a deal that says you won't have to ride her at all. All you'll be doing is the looking-after. Would – would that be too terrible?"

Nicky looked at Mum. He looked at Sabrina. He wanted to dance with them both around the nettles.

He wanted to climb in the trolley and whirl about the site with his arms stretched out to hug the world. He wanted to put wings on the trailer and fly them all to the moon and back.

"I'll probably survive," he said.

15

Courtney took Nicky to breakfast in the marquee.

Nicky looked round him while she went to get the food. Everything smelled of crushed grass and damp canvas. There were bench-tables everywhere, the pub garden sort. A flap in one side of the canvas led out to the catering trailer, and pink-faced staff were hurrying in and out with loaded trays.

Courtney came back and led Nicky to a table. "I'll pick you up every morning – just like I did today. Then we'll come straight here and eat. Richard says an army marches on its stomach. Everyone has to have a good breakfast, to set them up for the 'storm of action'." She put the tray down on the table and pushed it towards Nicky. His plate was loaded with bacon, eggs, tomatoes, mushrooms, fried bread and beans.

She had kept back a small pot of yoghurt for herself.

Nicky picked up his knife and fork and glanced across at her. "I reckon I'd end up carrying you into this battle. You'll never build your muscles on that."

Courtney fiddled with the crystal ring on her middle finger. "I'm not usually hungry first thing." She talked quickly, her thin fingers plucking at the buttons on her cardigan.

Her mood changed suddenly, and her thin face brightened, as Richard King and Dave the cameraman walked in and nodded at her.

They collected two plates piled high with sausages and bacon and went to sit at the other side of the tent.

Courtney turned back to Nicky. "Once you get to know everyone here, it's like one big happy family. We're all great friends."

Nicky watched her stirring her yoghurt with her spoon. She hadn't even started it yet. He finished another mouthful of beans and bacon. "So how did you get into this?"

"I was an extra first of all. That's someone in crowd scenes and things like that. I had – still have – an agent."

"Isn't it boring?"

"Not for me. I always wanted to act. I was always dressing up and doing plays when I was little. But I didn't have a proper family – I grew up in foster homes. When I left school I decided I wanted to look after children, and I ended up as a nanny for a TV presenter in London. Richard King came to dinner. I overheard him saying that he needed a chaperone for an American kid who was coming over to do a film here—"

"Does everyone need a chaperone?"

"It's the law in this country for anyone under sixteen."

Nicky pulled a face. Courtney was supposed to be his chaperone too, and he hated the idea of her following him around and watching him all the time.

"Don't look like that. I won't be breathing down your neck every second. I just need to know where you are, and that you're all right. Sort out all your problems. Make sure they don't work you too hard." She gave him a funny, excited little shrug. "I'll take you to meet people too. There's millions here. Richard King's the top director, but there's three assistant directors. Then there's people from Costume. People from Make-up. Designers. Lighting people. Camera people. Sound people. Like I said – one really big wonderful family..."

"I just want to do my job," Nicky said quickly. "I don't need all the rest."

Courtney stirred the yoghurt round the other way, her face snapping shut, "OK. But I'm here if you want me." She didn't look at Nicky, but she sounded as hurt as if he'd just refused to go to a tea party with her favourite sister.

He scanned the faces of people wandering in, trying to think of something else to say. "Do the actors have breakfast here too?"

"All of them except Elinora Moon. She's a bit of an odd-ball. She prefers to stay in her trailer between shoots. She doesn't even stay at the hotel like the others."

"Is Levi in a hotel?"

"He sleeps there, but he's got his trailer – well, it's really a bus – on site. He spends most of his time here." She fiddled absently with the ring. It seemed loose, as if it was about to fall off. Then she gave Nicky a real smile. It lit up her face, softening the sharp features. "He says he prefers the company."

"Richard King said Levi comes from California – from a ranch out there."

"That's right. Levi's told me all about it. It's a big place. Acres and acres."

"So what's he doing in this game?"

"He got discovered. A film company had gone to his family's ranch to make a documentary about breaking horses. They were really supposed to be talking to his dad, but they interviewed Levi too. When the programme went out a few months later, the TV company got bombarded with letters and phone calls – all from girls wanting to know more about him. Richard King got wind of it, and at the time he was looking for a boy to play the lead role in that last film – *Darkness*. He flew over to the States to audition him, and it just sort of grew from there." Courtney sighed, scooping a spoonful of yoghurt out of the pot and staring at it. "I suppose what happened to him is what the rest of us dream about."

Nicky shrugged. It wasn't what he dreamed about – not unless it was in a nightmare – but he didn't want to upset her again. But the thought of Levi living on a ranch bothered him. He'd heard they gave horses rough treatment at some of those places. "So – does Levi like the life? All the glitz and stuff."

"It's not all gold and glitter. Filming can be really boring. Richard can be a beast to work with. Everything gets shot over and over and over. Levi's used to hard work, but for the rest of it – I think it's a kind of game. He just goes along with it."

"Do you know him well then?"

Courtney nodded. She let the yoghurt drop back off the spoon and into the pot. "I worked with him on the last film We really got on. We sort of – understand each other."

Nicky squirted a dollop of tomato sauce on to his plate, then looked up suddenly. There was a change in the marquee. Everyone had stopped eating and talking. He stabbed a fried mushroom on to his fork, then turned round to see Levi Buick limping in through the entrance.

A cheer broke out, followed by clapping.

Levi nodded round at everyone, his eyes sliding over Nicky as if he was invisible. "Hey – cut it out." He held his hands up, his grin like a naughty schoolboy. "I only fell off."

Courtney tasted a tiny teaspoon of yoghurt, her eyes following Levi as he strolled casually past the tables, everyone reaching out to shake his hand or pat his back. She leaned across to Nicky. "He'll come over to us in a minute. I'll introduce you."

Nicky didn't let on that they'd already met. If Courtney didn't recognize him as the boy who'd messed up the shot that Friday after school, he wasn't about to remind her.

Levi walked on through the marquee. He walked straight past Nicky and Courtney as everyone clustered round him.

Nicky saw Suzy, the girl from the Props trailer, get up and give him a hug. She linked her arm through his and led him over to the table she'd been sitting at.

Courtney put her spoon down with a clatter. "Excuse me."

Nicky watched her go over to Levi. She bent over him. He gave a brief nod, and winked at her.

Suzy spread a thick film of honey inside a croissant. Her eyes stayed fixed on Courtney the whole time.

After a minute Courtney went and got Levi some breakfast.

She hovered behind him, watching him as he ate. Levi rolled up his sleeves and showed off his bruises to Suzy.

Courtney came back. She looked furious, flashing like an angry diamond, but she kept her voice even. "I told Levi you were here. Richard's already told him all about you. He said I should take you to see Starlight, and he'll come and see how you're coping later. She's not scheduled in till tomorrow morning, so you've got all of today to fix her."

Nicky scraped up the last of his baked beans and pushed his plate away. It bothered him that Courtney and Richard King seemed to think Starlight was just a damaged prop that needed sticking together, but he kept quiet. If they started thinking differently, he might not be here at all and – although he was still mad at Dad – the idea of seeing Starlight again had buzzed through his thoughts all night.

Nicky looked across at Levi again. He'd unbuttoned his shirt, and Suzy was acting out shocked horror as he showed her his bandaged chest. Nicky turned back to Courtney. "We'll go when you've finished eating."

Courtney had been watching Levi too. She suddenly pushed the uneaten yoghurt to one side. "I've finished already. Let's go now."

16

Nicky had expected to find Starlight in one of the big expensive trailers, or maybe a newly repaired stable from the old block where the carriage horses used to be kept.

But Courtney led him round the side of Chestnut Court, to where a stable door had been recently fitted to replace the original one. "In here," she said, pressing a series of buttons to open the coded padlock.

Nicky followed her in.

Starlight was right by the door, pushing her head into the crook of his arm as soon as he stepped inside. He felt the flash of excitement as he touched her. It was just like the other day. She made him feel different. She *was* different. Different from any other horse he'd ever met. Whatever else happened, it was great to be here.

Then he turned round, taking in for the first time the room he was in.

There was only one modern thing in the room – a heavy metal fire door on the far side, recently fitted, which led deeper inside the Court.

Other than that, the whole room was just like it would have been in the days when real royalty had been there. The walls were freshly painted in jade green. Trails of gold ivy patterned the edge nearest the ceiling, winding into the ornately carved stonework of leaves and flowers that decorated each corner. There were even yellow silk curtains at the windows – although the glass had been replaced by a metal grille.

From the ceiling hung a silver chandelier, the sparkling crystals catching the light with a dazzle of rainbows.

"Christ!" Nicky turned to Courtney in disbelief. "This is crazy."

"It's just a gimmick. Alexis – the publicity manager – thought it up, and the fans love it."

"But doesn't Levi *mind*?"

"Why should he? You wait until you see inside his bus. It's midnight-blue, with silver fittings and furniture. There's a laser display on the back that comes on when he plays CDs, and holograms of stars on the insides of the windows. It's not how he really lives – he only spends time in there for interviews and things. But it's part of the business. Part of the 'dream machine'. And it's not hurting anyone."

Nicky got a sudden flash of a dark, damp shed on the outskirts of Maybridge. "It must have cost a fortune to do this room out." He kicked at the straw that covered the floor. "I'm surprised it's not carpeted."

"Alexis did suggest it, but Levi said it wasn't practical. For obvious reasons."

"Surely kids would rather see Starlight living like a real horse than a – than a kind of four-legged princess."

Courtney pointed to an ornate cast-iron fireplace on the far side of the room. Fresh bouquets of flowers burst from silver vases nailed to the mantelpiece. The whole chimney-breast was pinned with cards and letters. "They don't seem to mind."

Nicky shook his head. Outside the metal grille a soft white dove puffed its chest, pecked its way along the window-sill, and flew off. "This isn't how a horse should be kept."

"But she's got everything she could ever want. The best food. The best tack. The best trailer for when we have to move her around. It keeps the fairy tale alive for her as well as for us."

Starlight snorted suddenly, pushing her nose into Nicky's shoulder. The touch of her bubbled through him again, lightening him up. He guessed Courtney was right, in a way. There wasn't really anything *wrong* with the way Starlight was living. It was the difference between this, and the way all the Dustys of the world had to live, that made it crazy. He rubbed Starlight gently between the eyes, then bent to run his hand down her bad leg. It had stiffened during the night and she'd be lame again by the evening if he didn't get on with it now. "I suppose I can work on her here just as well as I can anywhere else."

Courtney nodded distractedly. She seemed on edge – fiddling with her cardigan again and glancing over her shoulder. "You look like you're going to be OK for a bit. I'll go and see if I can find out what's happened to Levi."

17

Nicky stood with his back to the door. Lifting Starlight's hoof with one hand, he traced small rings just above it with the other, his own body moving with the pattern as he turned her leg in wider and wider circles. He'd done this before – it was one of the ways Grandad had shown him – but he wasn't just working from memory. He was working from instinct too, from the flow of feelings that moved out of Starlight and into him.

Suddenly Nicky heard footsteps scrunching through the leaves outside. They stopped, and there was the creak and rattle of someone leaning against the bottom half of the stable door. Nicky guessed it was Levi. He didn't look round, but knowing Levi was there changed him. He tensed. He felt awkward. The flow between him and Starlight seized up like a tap turning off. Starlight tried to pull her leg away.

There was a low whistle, then a girl's voice said, "Christ. This room's been done out like the inside of a palace! I can't believe it."

Nicky almost dropped Starlight's hoof on his foot. He turned round, amazed to see Bretta grinning in at him. He stared at her for a moment as if she'd just been beamed down from outer space. "What are you doing here?"

"I got sent an invitation."

"To what?"

"To come here. To spend the day. To see what goes on."

"You're lucky. From what I could see when I arrived, they've got armed guards on the gates." Nicky felt a sudden warmth at seeing Bretta. Having her around would be great. "Who invited you?"

Bretta's face flooded pink. "Levi Buick."

Nicky straightened up, his eyes level with hers. "Why?"

"Because of yesterday. I was the first one to reach him when he fell, and I stayed with him till the ambulance came. After that I sort of got dragged off and given a drink in the marquee and everything. You'd gone when I got back. But anyway – Levi remembered me. He went to loads of trouble to find out where I lived, and he even organized for a limo to pick me up this morning. He's so busy, and he'd had a horrible accident, so it was brilliant of him to make all that effort, don't you think?"

Nicky didn't answer. It annoyed him that she'd agreed to come. She wasn't interested in films, and superstars, and empty rubbish like that. This was the first day of half-term. She should be out racing through the leaves with Eclipse.

He walked round to Starlight's right foreleg. If the left one was bothering her, there was a chance she'd been putting extra pressure on the other one instead. He knelt down and ran his hands from her shoulder to her hoof. Starlight turned her head and nudged his shoulder, her body relaxing against him. Nicky felt the tension in her leg begin to fade. The energy was flowing between them again. Suddenly he turned back to Bretta and grinned. He was stupid to get so prickly. It was a chance for her to see what went on. "It's great you're around. Maybe we can stick together. I can talk you through what I'm doing with Starlight, and maybe we can go to lunch and stuff later."

Bretta hesitated. "It sounds great. I'd love to work with you and Starlight. But..."

"But no thanks." The lazy American drawl cut off her sentence. Levi sauntered up to the door, winking at Bretta, not even glancing at Nicky. "You're my star guest. I want you to spend time with me. I've got a whole film set to show you round."

Bretta smiled up at him, her face rushing pink again.

"So *you're* this 'horse wizard' Richard's been on about? The kid who tried to give mouth to mouth to a dummy last Friday afternoon?" Levi leaned his arms on the stable door, his eyes sliding lazily over Nicky.

Nicky pressed on Starlight's leg more fiercely than he'd intended. She flicked her tail, and pulled away in surprise.

"Watch how you treat that animal." Levi winked at Bretta again, then clicked his fingers. Immediately Starlight walked towards him, her ears pricked forward. "A three-legged horse won't be any use to me."

As Nicky watched Starlight rest her nose against Levi's shoulder he felt a rush of irritation, and the words came out before he could think what he was saying. "I thought three-legged horses were what you were used to. I thought that was how you broke horses where you come from. Tying up one leg till the horse is so mad with fear it'll give in to you for anything."

"Every man's way is different," Levi shrugged.

"Who's to say who's right and who's wrong?" He stepped back slightly, slapping Starlight's neck and grinning down at Bretta. She grinned back.

Nicky knew he should let it go, but Levi's indifference was somehow worse than a proper fight. "How could it ever be right to half-cripple a horse like that?"

"What my family does works fine with us. It's been working for generations. You can't compare the wild mustangs of America with the milk-fed horses you get over here—"

Nicky's voice was shaking now, and he walked up beside Starlight. "Even if you found horses on Mars, I bet they'd be the same, deep inside. Fear is part of what they are. So is the need to please. You work with one, I work with the other. And horses sense things in people. They know who's on their side."

Levi raised one eyebrow. "So how come this little horse isn't shivering in its shoes right now? And you watch me riding at the shoot tomorrow morning. There'll be nothing you could have done that I can't. Me and this horse are a team. We wouldn't have got to the top of the pile if we'd been anything else. So I guess you'd better start thinking about that."

Nicky turned away sharply. He hated the way Levi – his turquoise eyes dancing with amusement

– seemed to be laughing at him. And he didn't want to think about Levi riding Starlight either. The image of them both together cut into him like a knife. He ran his hand down Starlight's leg again, struggling to focus back on what he'd been doing.

He could feel Levi and Bretta still watching him.

"See you then Nicky," Bretta said softly. She sounded uncomfortable.

Nicky ignored her. He felt stupid. Like somehow, by not answering, he was putting himself in Levi's power. But he didn't trust himself to speak any more.

After a few minutes, Levi and Bretta walked away, Bretta dissolving into giggles at something Levi said about dummies.

Nicky kept working all day, refusing to join Courtney in the marquee for lunch, and trying not to let the storm of feelings inside him spoil his first day with Starlight.

18

"**S**he looks so magical. Like a dream horse." Courtney walked alongside Nicky as he led Starlight round to where the shooting had been scheduled to take place.

"She's not bad." Nicky's answer came out as not much more than a grunt, but Courtney was right. The way her coat glittered. The way she curved her neck and arched her steps. It was easy to see why all the horse-mad fans were nuts about her.

They rounded the corner into the grounds that ran along the back of Chestnut Court.

There were film crew everywhere. They were standing in clusters checking papers, checking monitors, talking to each other through hand-held radios.

Levi and Richard King were in the centre of everything. Richard King towering, his voice filling the air. Levi seeming brighter, more charming, and yet somehow separate from everybody else. Nicky watched him for a moment. He hated to admit it, but there was something about him. The way he stood. The way he tilted his head when he laughed. Even the way he constantly pushed the flop of fringe back casually from his eyes.

Nicky put his hand up to his own hair, and tilted his head.

Courtney frowned at him. "Have you hurt your neck?"

Nicky dropped his hand back down again. "Thought I felt a fly on my ear," he muttered.

"Take Starlight over near Richard and Levi," Courtney rushed on. "Costume and Make-up will need to check her over. Everything has to be perfect."

As he drew near, Nicky stole a glance at Levi. He was taking no notice of the little gathering of assistants who were fussing round him. Perhaps that was another part of what Levi did. Ignoring people. Perhaps it made people want him to notice them more.

Richard King was pacing backwards and forwards. He kept his eyes closed, as if he was playing out the scene in his head. "You'll be galloping along, heading towards the hedge. It's the part where Elinora seems to appear from nowhere. Remember you see her as something evil. Whenever she turns up bad things happen. I need you to think shocked, – scared – maybe a bit of blind panic. We'll be coming in as close as we can get to your face. Don't worry about the sound though. We'll be fixing that in post-production."

Levi nodded. "Are you doing the dummy bit today as well?"

Richard King swung round, opening his eyes and pacing the other way again. "I've planned that for the end of the week. We'll be mixing in computer graphics for the moment when you fall, but we want some action shots of you racing up to the tree first."

Levi grinned. "Didn't you shoot that on Sunday?"

"We got some of it, but Dave focused mainly on the horse. It was an opportunity we couldn't miss. Her expression was superb – especially the bit just before you fell. We could have spent hours trying to set that up."

Nicky turned away, leaning his back against Starlight's neck. He couldn't get a grip on this world where Starlight's fright was an "opportunity". She blew into his hair, relaxing against him, and he tried to relax with her. But it was so busy out here.

He would never have believed one small scene could need so many people.

Libby from Costume came over and checked Starlight's bridle.

Rachel from Make-up dabbed red paint on her neck and withers.

They both flicked smiles at Nicky, then went back to Levi.

Nicky spotted Elinora Moon over by the hedge, being fussed over the same way as Levi. The cats were with her, safely held on thin gold leads. Nicky could see the sudden sparkle of diamonds flashing out from their collars. Suddenly Elinora looked across at Nicky. It was a long look, and even from the distance between them Nicky got a sense of something he couldn't quite place. And when she turned away it was with such a heavy movement that it cut into him, almost frightened him.

Nicky flushed. Perhaps she was remembering how it was him who'd got in the way of the last two shots out here. Perhaps she'd heard he was a real Gypsy. Perhaps she thought he was bad luck. Quickly he dropped his own gaze. When he glanced up again she was walking away, the cats slinking like dusty grey shadows beside her.

Suzy appeared, hovering behind Levi. She was eating a giant bar of chocolate, and scribbling notes into a yellow plastic file. Courtney stood behind her, speaking into her mobile phone. Nicky saw them both look up, their eyes narrowing suddenly.

He followed the direction of their stare.

Bretta was getting out of a white limousine and hurrying towards them.

Suzy snapped her file shut and broke off another slab of chocolate.

Courtney finished her call.

"I'm sorry I'm late." Bretta ran over, her smile glittering at everyone. "I had a few problems with my horse, Eclipse. The chauffeur was brilliant though. He said Levi had told him..."

"Sssssssh," hissed Courtney. "We all need to listen to Richard."

Suzy pushed the remains of the chocolate bar into her pocket.

"OK." Richard King stopped pacing. "First rehearsal please."

The cluster round Levi hurried away, jostling for positions along the hedge. Levi spotted Bretta. He grinned suddenly and winked at her. She blushed and smiled. Courtney grabbed her arm and pulled her back towards the hedge with the rest of them.

Levi took Starlight from Nicky and vaulted on.

Nicky watched them trot away. Starlight moved well with him, and he looked good on her. Nicky wished he could find something wrong with the way Levi handled her, but he couldn't.

"What do I do now?" Nicky edged over to Courtney, hoping she could give him something else to do.

"Just stay around," Courtney kept her eyes locked on to Levi. "Find a place to watch from. They'll call you if they need you."

Nicky made his way up the steps and sat leaning against one of the tall stone pillars. From the corner of his eye he saw Bretta slip away from Courtney.

A moment later she appeared at the top of the steps. "It's great here, isn't it?"

"It's different."

"I never dreamed filming would be such hard work. Levi took me to watch them shoot another scene with Elinora this morning. Richard started bellowing because it wasn't going right. If it was me I would have just burst into tears, but Elinora stayed really calm. He made her go over and over it until they got it right. I suppose you have to be really tough to put up with it all."

Nicky glanced sideways at her. As she spoke, her eyes followed Levi who was galloping towards the gap in the hedge where Elinora was stepping out in front of them. Again. And again. And again.

Bretta seemed happy. As if she was lit up from the inside.

Nicky forced himself to watch Levi too. "He's

not like us," he said suddenly, his voice gruffer than he'd meant it to sound.

Bretta didn't seem to notice his tone. "I know. He's really interesting. He's been all over the world since he got famous. He knows about loads of things – not just horses. And he's great to be with. Do you know, he told me earlier this really funny story about..."

"But he's not like us with horses. Not like you and me."

"He grew up in a completely different sort of place. He's always had working horses. He's been trying to explain it to me. He says horses aren't pets to him, like they are to people like us..."

"I don't think of horses as pets." Nicky stabbed his thumb at some soft yellow moss that was growing round the base of the pillar. How could she say that? It was suddenly as if Bretta didn't understand anything about him.

"What I mean is, lots of the time Levi's horses don't even have names. He was telling me they're just 'the red horse' or 'the spotted horse'. All his family think like that. And perhaps if you'd owned hundreds of horses in your life, or had to grow up in that tough cowboy world, you might be more like that too."

"I doubt it." Nicky felt as if she was throwing rocks at him. He rolled the moss between his fingers, squashing it into a ball.

104

Below them, Starlight and Levi were galloping towards Elinora again.

Nicky turned back to Bretta. "So what's this film about?"

She hesitated. "Levi told me not to tell anyone..."

Nicky flicked the moss away, watching it scatter into dust. "I'd hate you to give away any of Levi's secrets." He saw Bretta stiffen beside him, and he was sorry. He didn't even know why he was so angry with her. Except that she suddenly seemed light-years away from him, and he didn't know what to do about it.

Down below Richard King shouted, "Going for a take now."

Somebody shouted, "Action."

Somebody thrust a clapboard in front of Starlight's nose.

Levi and Starlight galloped across the ground of Chestnut Court towards the gap in the hedge. Elinora stepped out suddenly.

Richard King roared, "OK. Cut. Let's take it again."

Nicky and Bretta shuffled further apart. Neither of them spoke.

A couple of times Nicky thought he felt Bretta glance at him, but he kept his eyes straight ahead. He could be like Levi Buick too. He could ignore people if he felt like it.

Nicky got up. He was bored. He'd go off for a while until they needed him again.

He hesitated for a moment, looking across at Bretta. All this scratchiness between them was stupid. He couldn't keep it up. She was supposed to be his best mate. "Do you want to come for a walk?"

But Bretta was leaning forward, her chin in her hands, watching Levi pass her again. And again. And again. She didn't even seem to realize that Nicky had spoken.

Nicky turned and walked away.

The ignoring people idea seemed to be about as successful as the head-tilting.

19

Nicky found a dark, shadowed corner round the back of Chestnut Court.

The building here had a derelict, forgotten look. The windows were all boarded up, and twined round with ivy. A long crack ran up one side of the wall. Lumps of fallen masonry littered the long grass. Everything was crumbling away.

Nicky settled against the wall, raking his fingers through a mound of rotting leaves and disturbing a woodlouse that rolled up immediately and played dead. Nicky gently sprinkled a handful of grass and twigs back over it. It had the right idea. Playing dead could keep you out of a whole lot of trouble.

"Where have you been?" Courtney appeared

suddenly, her voice cracking between worry and relief. "Levi needs you back with Starlight. Richard's just been roaring at me. I'm supposed to keep tabs on you all the time."

Nicky stood up, brushing away the dust and leaves from his jeans. "I thought they wouldn't be finished for ages."

"It's always like that." Courtney unpicked a thick thorn that had hooked itself on to her cardigan. "Richard decides he's got what he wants, and it's finished. I don't even know what it is that makes him decide that. It all looks the same to me."

"Me too." Nicky stood up.

Courtney looked more anxious than ever. Frail as a dry leaf, and as easily crushed. He was sorry Richard King had been growling at her because of him. He hated the thought of her having to know his every move, but she was only doing her job. And he hadn't missed her red puffy eyes and her blotchy cheeks. Courtney was obviously nowhere near as tough as Levi and Elinora.

They walked together round to the front of Chestnut Court.

"Oh – by the way..." Courtney stopped and rummaged in her bag suddenly. "These came for you." She handed Nicky a small stack of pastel-coloured envelopes.

"What are they?"

Courtney slanted a look at him. "Fan mail. Alexis in publicity gave them to me."

Nicky stared at them for a moment. He'd never had a letter in his life before. The closest thing he'd ever got had been when Bretta had sent him a map drawn on an old chocolate wrapper once. He realized Courtney was watching him curiously, and he crammed the envelopes into his jacket pocket. He didn't want to risk her suggesting he open them in front of her. "Why would anyone send me fan mail?"

"You were on telly Sunday evening. Half the country probably saw what you did with Starlight."

"It was only for five minutes." He followed her over to where Suzy was holding on to Starlight, patting her neck in the tense, jerky way people who never handle horses always touch them.

"It was a bit more than that. The publicity department did a follow-up the next night – there'd been so many phone calls about the whole incident. Lots of fans were going frantic about both Levi and Starlight, and it was important that they were reassured. They ran the news clip again, and said a bit more about you, too – about how you were working with Starlight now."

Nicky frowned. He had that same feeling again that he'd had the night Richard King had come to the trailer. The feeling that something was being taken from him. "Shouldn't they have asked?"

Courtney gave a short laugh. "You're public property, Nicky. We all are, potentially. Except that most of us don't do anything interesting enough for it to cause us a problem."

Nicky took Starlight's reins from Suzy. She wandered off, pulling the chocolate bar out of her pocket again. The thought of being described as "public property" made him even more bristly and uncomfortable. "But it's still crazy that people are sending me *fan* letters. It doesn't make sense. I had my back to the camera most of the time."

Courtney sighed, watching something across the grounds. "I don't think fans are known for being particularly sensible," she said quietly.

Nicky followed her gaze, to where Levi was telling Bretta something over by the gap in the hedge. Bretta flushed pink and giggled. Nicky didn't miss the sudden flash of light from her middle finger as a new crystal ring she was wearing caught the sun.

He tugged more sharply at Starlight's reins than he'd meant to, and led her away.

20

"Hey – fan mail!" Sabrina grabbed the bundle from where Nicky had dropped it on to the table. "Who are they from?"

"How should I know?" Nicky wandered over to Mum, who was fiddling with the knobs on the cooker. "Didn't that bloke fix this?"

Mum shook her head. "He doesn't seem to have. It'll have to be fish and chips again tonight."

Nicky took a Coke from the fridge and walked back in to Sabrina, slumping down on the seat.

"How was Levi?" Sabrina was almost bouncing beside him.

"He sends you his undying love."

Sabrina giggled, and nudged him. "Tell me the truth – did you go about with him? Is he funny? Do you think you'll stay friends even after the filming's finished?

Nicky took a swig of Coke. "Leave it, can't you? I'm knackered."

Sabrina's face fell for a moment, then she brightened again. "So aren't you going to open these letters?"

"I'm not bothered."

Sabrina looked at Nicky, her head on one side. "I'll read them with you," she said softly. "We'll sort them out between us. Take it in turns."

Nicky grunted, and Sabrina picked up two envelopes – one pink and one yellow. She handed the yellow one to Nicky, and pulled a card out of the pink one. "Dear Nicky," she read slowly, stumbling slightly, big gaps between the words. "I saw you calming Starlight down on the telly and I think you're great. Love Kate." Sabrina giggled. "Your turn."

Nicky looked down at the yellow envelope and pulled a face. "OK then. Just for you." He pulled at the folded paper on the inside, a soft smell of perfume leaking out. He read the words even more slowly than Sabrina had. "Dear Nicky, I loved seeing you and Starlight and the donkey and the puppy. You must be a very magical wonderful person. When is it your birthday? Love Laura."

Sabrina took another one. "Dear Nicky, I'm saving up to buy a horse one day. Could you send me a photograph to hang in my bedroom? You have beautiful eyes. Love Bethany."

"Dear Nicky, Could you send me a lock of your hair. I had a locket for Christmas and it is sad and empty. Just like me. I keep thinking about you. What is your favourite pop group? Love Emily." Nicky looked up at Sabrina. "How do real stars have time for all this rubbish? They must get thousands of these each week."

There was one letter left. It was a deep-purple envelope. There was no name on the front, but the sender had drawn a picture of a golden horse all sparkling with stars. A dark-haired boy with a donkey was walking towards it. It was an odd picture – the colours and proportions unusual and wild – but the boy was obviously meant to be Nicky. He opened it carefully.

"What is it?" asked Sabrina. "What does it say?"

Nicky shook his head, scrunching it fiercely in his fist. "A load of rubbish. Like the rest of them." He picked the whole lot up suddenly, and grabbed a box of matches from the kitchen. "I'm going out for a while," he said to Mum. "Tell Dad I'll be about an hour."

Outside, he went over to the supermarket trolley.

Then, wiping the inside dry with the sleeve of his jacket, he dropped the letters in slowly, one by one, and struck a match against the envelopes.

They burned quickly, crumbling without protest into ashes.

Nicky saved the purple envelope till last.

It took longer to catch. Small yellow flames crept nervously along the edges, curling to lick the horse's legs, then its body. As its head began to burn the whole thing flared up suddenly, a fierce angry flame that hissed and crackled over the felt-penned Nicky and Dusty.

When it was over. Nicky pushed the dead grey cinders through the bottom of the trolley with a stick. He wanted everything gone. Everything forgotten.

It should have been easy. Usually he forgot about stuff he'd read at school. He hated being given words to learn for school assemblies because he couldn't ever remember them. He had special books to read at school – all part of a reading scheme that most of the others had left behind years before – but even though they were supposed to be simple it was still a battle to get through them.

But this letter wouldn't go away. The words had been jumbled. Untidy. As if the sender wasn't much better at writing than Nicky. And he didn't properly understand it. He only knew that it was weird. Weird. Something to be scared of. And as he ran off across the site, the message seemed to go with him. Locked in his head.

I'VE BEEN WAITING FOR YOU.

21

The dogs had all been shut away for the night. There was occasional barking from inside the house as Nicky scrunched up Maddy's leaf-strewn drive, but Maddy didn't come out. Nicky wasn't bothered. He'd maybe knock on the door later, but just now he wanted some time with Dusty, and to have something else to think about.

He pulled up the collar of his jacket, bent slightly against the wind that ripped round the corner of the house, and turned into the yard.

As he drew near the stable he heard voices. A sudden giggle. Bretta. Nicky felt an odd relief. He'd been stupid that afternoon – really messed things up between them – and this was a chance to put it right. And maybe he'd tell her about the letter too.

She could help him sort out what he ought to do about it.

He paused for a moment. She was chatting to Dusty as if he was one of her greatest friends. Nicky grinned to himself. It was great that Bretta had gone in there on her own. And great that Dusty was letting her be with him.

He stepped closer, reaching for the torch that Maddy always kept tucked on a ledge under the eaves, ready to surprise Bretta.

"You have to do as little as you can. You try to let the animal have a feeling of control. If he starts to look as if he's not handling it you have to stop until he's ready again."

Nicky leant back in the shadow of the wall. She was almost word-perfect. She really had been listening to him. And now she must be passing it on to Maddy. He felt strange for a moment, hearing his words come out of Bretta's mouth like that. But he'd been doing the right thing – sharing what he knew. It was crazy to lock it all up as if it was some enormous secret. Bretta would pass it to Maddy, and Maddy would pass it to someone else. More and more people would learn, and more and more horses and donkeys might have better lives because of it.

Bretta was still chattering on. "And there's no rules. It's different with each animal. That's why you have to spend a bit of time at the beginning, trying to get the feel of what's wrong. But I think that – as long as you really *want* it to work – then it will."

It felt, suddenly, as if all of the muck of the day just rose out of Nicky like steam. He felt warm suddenly. Almost glowing. He stepped forward, grinning. It was time to let them both know he was here.

And then he heard the second voice, and all the brightness inside him seemed to collapse in on itself.

"Hey – you really are some girl." Levi's drawl was unmistakable. "I'm not sure I go along with it all, but I'm willing to listen. Maybe you could teach me some more..."

Nicky clenched his fists until his knuckles cracked. So Bretta wasn't as careful with his secrets as she was with Levi's. He put his hand out to wrench open the stable door – and then stopped. What could he do? What were they doing wrong? It was everything, and nothing.

Bretta giggled again. Nicky heard Levi say something else – he couldn't work out what.

And suddenly he turned, running back through the storm of leaves that whipped and whirled across the shadowed garden, chasing him back out on to the road.

22

Nicky went in to work on Starlight the next morning. She'd stiffened up a bit in the night – Nicky could feel the tightness in her shoulder. But there was plenty of time. She wasn't scheduled to work till the following day.

He looked round the room. There was plenty of space, and he needed to watch how she trotted and walked. Outside would have been better. Riding her would have been better. But the deal Dad had done with Richard King was clear, and it wasn't worth the risk.

He stood under the chandelier, and drove Starlight in a circle round him. She went willingly – she was a performance horse and she did what she was told – but Nicky could sense she wasn't right.

"OK. Stand now." Nicky went closer to her. He could work on her, just touching and listening, but he wanted to try something different. It was something he'd seen Grandad do, but something he'd never had the guts to have a go at himself. It wasn't that it was difficult. It was just that he might look a bit of a prat if anyone was watching.

He went to the window and glanced through the metal grille.

There was nobody about.

Only a white dove that fluttered up suddenly, soaring away into the sharp blue sky.

Nicky went back to Starlight. "Walk on." She moved forward immediately. Behind her, Nicky walked too.

"Trot..." Nicky broke into a run, driving her in a tight circle. She was limping now – it was easy to see – and as she moved she twisted her neck awkwardly, as if she was trying to shift the balance of her weight. Nicky did the same, dragging his left leg and twisting his own head. Grandad said it always worked. Copying a horse's movements helped to pick up on the animal's mood. And it was working. Nicky's own back felt stiff, a tightness running from his left shoulder down to a dull ache in his leg.

"And walk." Nicky kept Starlight moving, changing her direction and following her again. He began hunching his left shoulder in the way she was hunching hers. Once she flicked her tail at the same moment that Nicky felt a light touch between his shoulders. An insect had landed on Starlight's back.

A card fell unexpectedly from the mantelpiece. Starlight jumped sideways, startled. Nicky felt the jump like a bird flapping suddenly in his chest, and then laughed out loud. This was great. It was crazy and weird, and he could never tell anyone about it, but it really worked. All he had to do was to learn how to flicker his ears.

"What are you doing – practising for one of your little British pantomimes?" The lazy drawl stopped Nicky like a lasso dropping round him. "What end are you going for? Front or back?"

"I'm listening to invisible signals." Nicky brushed imaginary dust off Starlight's neck.

Levi gave him that lopsided grin. "Who from – little green men?"

Nicky didn't answer. He wished he hadn't said anything. Even to him it suddenly sounded stupid.

Levi shrugged suddenly, as if he was already bored. "I came over to check on the horse – and to give you this."

"What is it?"

"Mobile phone. Elinora suggested it. It means we can contact you if you disappear again. It's dead simple. Press the green button to turn it on, and the red to turn it off. The rest of the instructions are in the box. Do you want to read them through now? Make sure it makes sense?"

Nicky took the package that Levi held out to him. He bet Bretta had told Levi he couldn't read. He was probably just having a laugh. "I'm busy here. I'll look at it later."

"So when d'you reckon you'll be done?"

"Maybe a couple of hours."

Levi flicked at a beetle that was scurrying along the edge of the door frame. "Richard's done with me for today, and there's nothing scheduled for Starlight. I've got a friend coming over with her horse later, and we're riding out together. She's been begging me to let her ride Starlight. So I thought we'd do a swap. And I reckon a change of scene would do this animal good, don't you?"

Nicky didn't answer. He didn't need to ask who Levi's "friend" was.

And he didn't want to think about Levi on Eclipse.

Bretta on Starlight.

All four of them off somewhere together.

He turned away, putting the package down in the straw and bending to massage Starlight's leg.

It wasn't until he'd heard Levi's footsteps scrunch away that he picked it up again and flung it hard.

It hit the vase with the white carnations.

The flowers trembled, a small flurry of petals fluttering like soft white feathers on to the straw.

23

Nicky wasn't supposed to go anywhere without telling Courtney, but he didn't care. He had the phone now. She could ring him when she wanted him. It was still working because he'd tried it after he'd picked it back up – stupidly ringing Bretta's home number even though he knew she wasn't in.

He didn't plan to go far. He'd stay within five minutes' walk of Chestnut Court. If Courtney called him he could be back in the grounds before she had time to worry about it. But it felt good to be out. Good to be walking away. Good to be gone before Levi and Bretta came for Starlight.

He walked along the track at the back of Chestnut Court. It twisted to the right, running along the edge of the field. Nicky went faster as he passed the padlocked five-barred gate. There were a few people stacking wood in the far corner ready for the fireworks shoot that night. Further away, half hidden by the hedge, Nicky thought he saw someone standing between the trees.

Just past the gate the track forked sharply, the left-hand turn dipping away into a small wood.

Nicky decided to follow it. The trees would give him decent cover and he wouldn't have to worry about being seen.

It wasn't exactly a picnic spot. He passed the blackened remains of a fire. Empty beer cans littered the ground. A nearby stream was blocked with crisp packets and bits of paper. Nicky poked the stagnant water with a stick, watching it swirl suddenly as the rubbish broke away. Then he walked deeper into the wood.

The trees grew denser.

He found a fallen log and sat down between soft grey fungus and crisp yellow leaves.

It was very quiet. From somewhere nearby a dove called softly.

A rabbit scuttered by, lit for a moment by a thin slant of sunlight that fell between the branches, turning it into a creature of gold. Then it was gone, melting back into the shadows again.

Suddenly the phone went. It had a twittering

ring. A tinny bright tune. A stupid, alien sound. For a moment Nicky couldn't remember which pocket he'd put it in. Then he couldn't work out which way up to hold it. Then he couldn't remember which button to press. And all the time the tinny bright tune twittered on and on. At last Nicky sorted it out. "Hello."

The line crackled.

"Courtney, is that you?"

The line crackled again. Nicky could hear breathing, and an odd sort of hushing sound.

"D'you need me for something?"

There was more breathing. More hushing. Then a voice spoke – and it wasn't Courtney. It was someone younger – much younger – sounding very far away. "I'm still waiting for you. I won't let you leave me again."

Then the line went dead.

24

Nicky stood up slowly.

The wood seemed darker. There were twisted shapes. The trees had faces. The branches had long fingers that could snag and catch.

He walked backwards, his eyes scanning the shadows. A trailing root caught the back of his trainer, sending him stumbling against the trunk of a giant oak.

Suddenly his foot sank, as if the ground was falling away. Water soaked into his trainer and the bottom of his jeans. He'd stepped into the stream. The cold shock startled him to his senses and he turned quickly. He knew where he was now. He was nearly back out at the track.

Then he heard a shriek, "There he is!"

Three girls sprang towards him.

The first – the tallest – thrust her autograph book at him.

The second stared as if he was an angel who'd just drifted down from the clouds.

The third just hugged herself tightly, and groaned.

25

The three girls followed Nicky back towards Chestnut Court.

"Can I have your autograph?" The tallest girl was walking so close to Nicky that their elbows touched.

Nicky pushed his hands deep in his pocket and stared straight ahead. There was no way he'd show himself up by writing his name in her stupid book. Supposing she asked him for something else. Supposing she suddenly wanted him to add on a message.

He stepped away, trying to get some space from her. She stepped with him.

The second girl closed in on his other side. "*Please* Nicky. We saw you on the telly. We think you're great."

Behind him, Nicky could hear the footsteps of the third girl. He walked faster.

"We'll go away if you just sign our books."

"Or give us a photograph."

"Or a lock of your hair."

"Look." Nicky stopped suddenly, facing them. "I'm not a film star. I'm not famous. I just work with horses and got on the telly for five minutes because I was in the right place at the right time."

"I wouldn't give you any trouble."

"I only want to be your friend."

"I *love* the way you speak."

Nicky closed his eyes, wishing Courtney was around to get rid of them. He pulled the phone out of his pocket, and then hesitated. If he told her what was going on he'd have to admit he'd left the grounds. He looked back at the girls again. "You don't know anything about me. I'm just..."

Suddenly someone stepped out from a break in the hedge. "Are these girls bothering you?"

"I..." Nicky turned round, startled, to find himself face to face with Elinora Moon, her three cats beside her on their thin gold leads. "They – they..." His voice trailed away. The girls were a pain, but he didn't want to drop them in trouble.

Elinora Moon nodded. "I thought so." She turned on the girls, her voice very soft. "None of you should be here. There are signs up everywhere to keep people away. But if you can promise to give Nicky some space, the casting director is still looking for extras for the fireworks scene tomorrow night. There's someone dealing with it round by the front gate. Why don't you see if you can put your names down?"

The girls nodded nervously, then turning together and breaking into a giggling run, they headed off towards the front gate.

Elinora Moon turned to Nicky, pushing her long hair back from her face. "After all these years, I'm still never sure of the best way to deal with fans like that."

"Thanks. It was getting a bit difficult." Nicky stared at the ground, feeling clumsy and awkward. Those girls had just been being stupid about him, but Elinora Moon really *was* famous.

"I know what it's like. When I first started to get known I was scared to death of everyone. People seemed to think they owned me. They were always touching me. Wanting things from me. Sending me things."

Nicky looked at her properly for the first time. She had a great face. Not pretty, but beautiful. Mysterious green eyes and dark wild hair. Close up, he could tell she must be about Mum's age, but he could see why everyone still went crazy about her. Yet there was something else about her. A trace of sadness that seemed to hover over her. Nicky was puzzled by it. How could anyone with so much going for them be sad?

She smiled at him. "Look, I've just finished walking these three, so why don't you come back to my trailer for a while? Richard's not shooting Starlight today, and you don't want to hang around on your own at the moment. A bit of company could do you good."

Nicky hesitated. He wouldn't normally go off with a gorgio he didn't know, but she wasn't exactly a stranger. He felt comfortable with her too. She was easy to talk to. And she was right. He would be safer being with her than he would be on his own.

26

"This is great!" Elinora's trailer took Nicky's breath away. It was more Gypsy-ish than any trailer he'd ever seen.

Elinora unclipped the cats' leads and they slipped away from her, slinking along the edges of the seats and cupboards as she ran water into a copper kettle. Nicky could see her eyes watching him from the ornate mirror above the sink. "I had all the modern cupboards and things pulled out. The only really new thing I've got is that tape player. I've never been able to –" She stumbled on the words for a moment, as if she'd been about to let Nicky in on a secret and then changed her mind. "My eyesight's not good. I learn all my scripts by tape."

She lifted one of the cats up from a pale lilac chair and nodded for Nicky to sit down.

The cat sat on the floor and stared at Nicky. Then it sprung up suddenly on to his knee. Nicky let it sniff his fingers. "I don't know much about cats. We've never had one. Gypsies almost never do. They don't fit in with the travelling life."

"We never had cats when I was growing up either. I've had to learn all about them. Now, I'm really tuned in to them. Some days, I can almost see what they're thinking." Elinora carried a tray over, set with purple china cups and delicate silver spoons, and sat down opposite Nicky. "I love getting inside the heads of animals. When I was your age my real passion was—" She broke off abruptly, the sense of sadness seeming to deepen for a moment. Then she brightened again. "So tell me all about your life. What's it like being a real Gypsy?"

Nicky shrugged, rubbing the cat's ears and chin. "It's not like anything really. It's just how I've always been."

Elinora nodded, pouring the tea, as if his answer made perfect sense to her.

Nicky rubbed the cat's ears, feeling its purring vibrations run up through his fingers. He looked round the trailer again, searching for something new to say. There were a couple of framed pictures in a glass cabinet – not proper pictures, but a child's paintings of horses galloping. They were odd. The horses were strange colours, and their bodies too long and too tall. But they had an energy that Nicky liked. He nodded at them. "They're good."

"They were a present. A little girl left them behind after she'd been to visit here once. I didn't see her to thank her for them. She came while I was out."

"I can't draw, but my sister can. She's brilliant. Not just horses, but all kinds of animals."

"Sometimes it runs in families. But..." Elinora passed a cup to Nicky. "You do have a special gift don't you? With horses, I mean."

The second cat sprang on to Nicky's other knee, curling itself across the first.

The two cats gazed deep into Nicky's eyes and purred.

Nicky shrugged. "I just grew up with horses. My grandad's good with them too. It was him who taught me everything."

The third cat jumped up silently and stretched along the back of the seat.

Elinora leaned forwards, her voice suddenly urgent. "It's so special to have a gift like that. Your family must be proud of you."

Nicky looked at her. He had the feeling that, if he suddenly told her everything, she'd understand. "My dad doesn't like horses much."

Elinora was watching him as closely as the cats. "I suppose that must have caused lots of rows between you."

Nicky glanced at her quickly. It was odd the way he didn't mind her knowing things about him. Twenty minutes ago, with those three girls, he'd hated them thinking they had the right to walk along the same bit of track as him. But now, here he was sharing his family secrets with a gorgio stranger. "You could say that."

"So – have you never had a horse of your own then?"

Nicky frowned. No one had ever asked him that question before. And he'd never even thought about it. It was such an impossible dream. "No."

Elinora put her head on one side and slanted a look at him. "It seems such a waste."

Suddenly a tinny bright tune began twittering from Nicky's jacket pocket. The cats sprang up and leaped across the trailer, glaring at Nicky as if he'd made his phone ring just to annoy them. At least this time Nicky had the hang of how it worked. He put it to his ear nervously, remembering the last call. "Hello?"

"Nicky." It was Courtney's voice. "Where *are* you? I've just been over to Starlight. I thought you'd be there."

Nicky glanced at Elinora. She wasn't looking at

him. She was staring past him, lost in some far away thought. Nicky had a hunch that his being in her trailer was best kept as a secret. "I'm – I'm having a break."

The three cats stared at him.

"Levi came back half an hour ago," Courtney rattled on. "He told me to tell you Starlight needs tidying up. But you ought to eat first. Shall I meet you outside the marquee?"

Nicky glanced out of the trailer window. There were people wandering into the marquee. He could make out Richard King, and Dave the cameraman. Behind them trailed Suzy. Suddenly he saw Bretta and Levi. Bretta was riding Levi piggy-back. Nicky could hear her squeals and giggles even from Elinora's trailer. "I'm not hungry. I'll skip lunch and get on with doing Starlight. Call me again when you're ready for her." Nicky pressed the red button on the phone and stood up.

Elinora switched back on to him. "Is the real world calling?"

Nicky nodded. "Something like that."

She walked with him down the steps of her trailer. "I hope you didn't think I was prying into your family. I've tried to research Gypsies as much as I can for this part, but there's nothing like talking to the real thing."

"It's been fine. And if you hadn't come along, I

might be pressed and glued into somebody's scrapbook by now."

Elinora squeezed his arm. "Look after yourself then. I'll be watching out for you."

As Nicky turned away he seemed suddenly lighter than he'd felt all week. She'd been good to talk to. And it struck him suddenly that Elinora was the opposite of Levi – dark and quiet, turned in on herself.

He decided that he really liked her.

If he had to have someone watching him, it wasn't so bad if it was her.

27

The film shoot the next morning started badly. Starlight wouldn't go down the steps between the hedge.

Nicky watched as Levi turned her at it again – and again – and again.

Courtney hurried over to Richard King. "You've got to stop this. We can't risk another accident."

Richard King glanced at his watch, then turned to Nicky. "What's she doing? Why's she like this?"

Nicky shook his head. "She was OK when I led her out." He glanced sideways at Bretta, who was watching Levi and chewing her lip nervously. Part of him wanted to believe it was something she and Levi had done on that ride out yesterday, but however hard he tried, it didn't fit. He couldn't see

Levi taking big risks with his co-star, and whatever he felt about Bretta at the moment, he knew she'd never do anything stupid with a horse.

Richard King glanced at his watch again, then jumped sideways as Starlight skittered backwards. "Get yourself off," Richard King let out a roar that sent Starlight skittering the other way. "Let Nicky have her."

Levi cantered Starlight in a slow circle. "I can handle this."

"That's not the point." Courtney twisted her fingers anxiously. "We need to keep you in one piece."

Levi raised his eyebrows and looked down at Nicky. "Supposing he gets hurt. Doesn't it matter?"

"Of course it matters." Courtney pushed her fingers through her hair. "But Nicky's different. He doesn't actually ride her. We can get him out of the way if anything goes wrong."

Suzy came forward with her file under one arm. "Come on." She popped a mint cream into her mouth, and offered one to Levi. "I can ask you some questions for my assignment while you're waiting."

Levi shook his head, and trotted Starlight round her.

Bretta ran up. "You could just have a rest for five minutes. We could sit by the hedge and let you catch your breath. It must be really hard work going over and over it like that."

Levi looked at her for a moment, then grinned suddenly. "You're right. I could do with a break." He sprung down and tossed Nicky the reins. "I'm here if you need me, kid."

Nicky led Starlight a little way off. He hated the others all being there watching. He ran his fingertips along Starlight's back. She shied sideways from him. She wasn't responding any better to him than she had done for Levi.

Richard King prowled round him. "Do you want me to call the vet?"

From the corner of his eye Nicky saw Levi and Bretta settle under an oak tree near the hedge. Levi began flicking acorns into the air, spinning them up with one hand and catching them with the other. Bretta giggled and tried to copy him. She dropped every one.

Nicky walked round to the other side of Starlight. He wasn't even sure what it was he was doing. He just knew he had to look like he had a plan. But the truth was, his mind was only half on the job. Levi's spinning acorns and Bretta's giggles were getting to him.

He took a deep breath, pressing his hands deep against Starlight.

On the terrace above him he saw Elinora watching. She made a slight movement – just a light nod of recognition. He nodded back, moving round to touch Starlight's forehead. And then suddenly it happened. Something Nicky had never felt before. A bubbling tension seemed to rise up under his skin. He felt dizzy. Not ill, but very light. Everyone around seemed distant and faint. He saw greens and gold-browns flash past him. He felt a weight on his back. Something hard in his mouth. From the corner of his eye he could see something rolling along beside him. He knew what it was – he'd seen it before – but he couldn't put a name to it. It didn't *have* a name. Nothing had a name. There were noises. Smells. He was moving fast – faster than he'd ever moved. A shadow streaked past. Something yelped, leaping out in front of him. He tried to twist away but he stumbled. Skidded. The weight on his back was leaning. It frightened him. It felt all wrong. Something scratched his face. He felt a searing pain in his leg.

And then it was over.

"Christ!" Nicky ran his hand across his brow, looking round at everyone, expecting someone to say something. Richard King was checking his watch against Dave's. Levi was still spinning acorns for Bretta. Courtney and Suzy were scowling across at them from over by the steps. Elinora and the cats were gone.

"How's it going?" Richard King strode over to him.

"Fine. I..." Nicky swallowed hard, struggling to sound normal. "I know what's wrong."

Richard King nodded impatiently. "What do we need to do?"

"We have to find another way to get her into the field. She won't go down the steps because she remembers that the last time she did this shot it ended with her getting hurt. I need to try and break the memory."

Richard King paced the length of the hedge, then walked back. "There isn't another way through."

"If you want to get that scene shot, you'll have to make one."

Richard King gave him a long stare. "If your idea doesn't work..."

Nicky stroked Starlight's nose. He knew his idea would work. He knew because a few minutes ago the field had smelt different. He knew because a few minutes ago he'd sensed odd shapes and sounds. But most of all he knew because, as the scene had flashed through him, he'd seen two figures standing, then running towards him. One of the figures – a slightly-built, dark-haired boy – had a donkey trotting behind him. And that could only mean one thing. A few minutes ago, Nicky had actually got inside Starlight's mind.

He turned back to Richard King. "Trust me."

28

Once the new gap had been made it didn't take long.

Nicky knotted Starlight's reins and let her follow him through into the field. It was just as he'd thought. Along a different route, she was fine.

He walked her over to the tree, leading her all round it, taking her in amongst the branches. Nicky lowered one down, letting it brush against her neck. She sniffed it for a moment and then lost interest.

Then, using the back of his hand, he pressed her all over, watching the ripples of colour flow out from her as she relaxed completely.

"She'll be OK now." Nicky walked her back to the steps where Richard King was waiting.

Libby brushed some dead leaves off Levi's shirt.

Rachel checked the red make-up on Starlight's shoulder.

Dave rolled the camera into place.

The shooting began.

Even Nicky could see it was going well. And for once, he didn't even mind seeing Starlight with Levi. He knew he had something special with her. Something Levi would never come close to. As he watched them do that wild gallop towards the tree he felt stupidly proud – like he was big and bright and full of buzzing light and energy.

"That's all. Thank you." Richard King stopped them abruptly, glanced at his watch, then went off to watch the re-run on the outside monitor.

"I think that was a record," said Courtney, hurrying over to Levi. "You did that in less than twenty minutes."

Levi vaulted off of Starlight and threw the reins at Nicky without even looking at him. Nicky didn't care. He knew now the rush of sound that filled a horse's ears. He knew now the way things were all shapes and smells. He knew now there could be a different feel to the ground beneath his feet.

Nicky didn't know if he'd ever have that happen to him again – if he'd ever manage to get inside a horse's head like that – but the memory of it would stay with him for ever.

From behind him, Nicky heard Bretta's voice,

"You were great. That was fantastic." Nicky felt a flood of warmth. She must have noticed he was different. Later, if he could get her on her own, he'd tell her about it. It was too big a thing to keep to himself.

He turned to grin at her – and then stopped.

Bretta wasn't even looking at him. She was laughing, sharing a joke with Levi. The others joined them, Courtney and Suzy patting Levi on the back. Even Dave and Richard King walked over to shake his hand.

And suddenly, for Nicky, everything went flat. There was more space around him than the freezing cold emptiness Miss Ekins said stretched between galaxies.

29

"Aren't you coming to be an extra at this fireworks thing?" Sabrina turned off the hair-drier and looked at Nicky as if she suspected he'd been taken over by an alien species. "You might never get the chance to be in a film again."

Nicky shrugged. "I never go to the cinema anyway."

"But half of Maybridge will be there. It'll be great."

"I've been at Chestnut Court all day. I've had a gutful of it."

Nicky looked out of the window as a van drew up outside. Two men got out carrying an enormous box. A new cooker for Mum.

Dad dropped a brochure about the latest in

pick-up trucks on the table and went to let them in. He came back a few minutes later, after they'd gone. "If you're not going with your sister you can give me a hand after I've dropped her off. I want to give the old pick-up a good going over. Jim's lined up a couple of blokes to come and look at it tomorrow.

"I've had a long day."

"Me too," Dad growled back. "All you've been doing is polishing up that horse. Me and Jim have been out doing—"

"Go on – finish it," Nicky spun round to face him. "You were going to say 'proper work', weren't you? You've got a new cooker, and you're planning for a new truck, on the back of what I've been doing. But you'd still rather I'd been out sawing wood and sweeping leaves."

"You'll have to get back to it after tomorrow, once that film lot's gone." Dad picked up the brochure and began flicking through it. "You'll be back in the real world then."

"So – now there's no big money to be made with horses, you can get your old rule-book out again, is that it?"

Dad swung round at Nicky. "It doesn't seem to me like a week with a horse has done you a lot of good. You've had a face like a wet weekend the whole time, and you're still talking to me like I'm the insect that got squashed on the sole of your trainer. Give me one good reason why I should let you go do it again."

Nicky pushed his hands deep in his pockets and stared out of the window. Dad was right – it had been a lousy week, but that wasn't to do with Starlight. Starlight had been the one good thing about it all.

And after tomorrow, she'd be gone.

Nicky hadn't let himself think about what that meant before, but suddenly the ache of her going pressed like a bruise on his chest. He'd never met a horse like Starlight, and the things he'd done with her – the way she'd let him into her mind – he couldn't imagine ever being able to do again. It was like he'd had a glimpse of a different world, and after tomorrow he'd have to hand the telescope back.

"I said, give me one good reason."

Nicky had forgotten Dad was there. "For what?"

"For me letting you work with horses again."

Nicky stared at Dad as if he was just swimming back into focus. "How about because I don't want to end up like you – just cutting trees, sawing logs, and becoming an old misery by the time I'm forty."

"If this life's not good enough for you, you can damn well take your chance somewhere else. Go and hang about with the homeless gorgio kids who sit around with a fleabitten dog and a begging bowl."

"Sounds like it might be more fun than living here." Nicky said it quietly, but Dad heard him.

He slammed the brochure down on to the table and grabbed Nicky's sweatshirt. His face, close to Nicky's, was distorted with rage. "Get out until you've come up with a better way to speak to me..."

"Suits me fine!" Nicky pushed Dad's fist away, glared round at Mum and Sabrina, and left.

30

Nicky didn't go far.

He stood swinging the pale beam of Maddy's torch round Dusty's stable, and listening to the whine and whirl of fireworks across the field. He wished now that he'd hung around for long enough to eat whatever Mum might try out in her new cooker. But he wouldn't go back now. Not yet, at any rate. He'd give Dad something to sweat about.

Dusty had no problem with the fireworks. Colours flickered in through the stable door. Great fizzes and bangs cracked the sky. The donkey stood sleepily, nuzzling Nicky's shoulder, as if he was puzzled about why Nicky had woken him up.

Maddy was indoors with all the dogs. Nicky could picture them all clustered round her, scrabbling to get close. He hoped Mum had remembered that Sky didn't like fireworks either.

Nicky left Dusty and walked back out into the yard.

He thought about Starlight. He wondered if she was OK. He knew she'd been trained like a police horse, but he had a bad feeling – a restless unease that seemed to drift with the smoke across the field.

The fireworks grew wilder. Strings of colour leaped and curled through the darkness. A spray like shining chrysanthemums floated silently to the ground. Pinks and blues twisted and whirled, calling to each other in tiny soft whimpers.

And then Nicky's phone rang. The child again. Her voice was crackling. Very distant. It was hard to hear above the noise. "*You have to come. I'm waiting for you.*"

Nicky felt ice-cold. "Who are you? What do you want?"

"*I'm waiting for you, Nicky. I've been waiting a long time.*"

"I'm not coming anywhere. Not until I know who you are."

"*Nicky. It's important. It's not just me. I've...*" The voice was drowned by a burst of firecrackers from across the field. And with it came a giant dazzle of light, silver crystals sparkling like exploding chandeliers beneath the ceiling of the sky.

And amongst the glittering colour and cracking sound Nicky heard the whispered name "...*Starlight*." It came out like a hiss. Something creeping. Something dangerous. And he didn't need to hear any more. It was almost as if he'd been waiting for it. Shining the torch in front of him he ran, vaulting over Maddy's gate and racing across the field as if some dark terrible monster was sucking him there.

31

Sabrina was right. Half of Maybridge had turned out for their five minutes of fame. They crowded into the grounds and spilled across the field.

"Hi Nicky." Matthew and Liam Frazer, who worked at the stable where Bretta kept Eclipse, waved across at him.

"Nicky!" A small girl dived out at him. "Shall I write your name with this sparkler?" It was Emily Hobbs – the daughter of a carpenter Dad sometimes did work for. "Some other time, Emily," Nicky said, straining a smile at her. He threaded his way on through the crowd.

"Hey – Nicky!" Billy Clarke and a couple of others from school loomed up. They crowded round him, clapping him on the back.

"Got to go," Nicky ducked past them. "I've got something to sort out."

"Nicky – Nicky –" The three girls who'd followed him that afternoon appeared from nowhere. Nicky slipped behind a man with a giant bunch of metallic gold balloons, all in the shape of horses' heads. The three girls disappeared again, jostled away by the crowd.

He saw Bretta, standing back from the others with Sabrina and Jade. She didn't see him, but she seemed lost. As if she was looking for someone.

There was no sign of Levi. Nicky guessed it was a security thing. There'd be a riot if he showed up on a night like this.

At last Nicky got to where the crowd was thinner. He turned the corner and headed across to Starlight's room.

Her door was bolted. Nicky was relieved. He'd half expected to see it swinging open – and Starlight gone.

He shone the torch on the lock, tapped out the code, and went inside.

It was very dark. Nicky flicked the beam round the edge of the room, calling softly. Starlight usually came over straight away. Tonight there was nothing. Just the sound of his own breathing, and his feet scuffling the straw.

Nicky smacked his fist against the wall suddenly.

Whatever had happened to Starlight, he was too late.

He pulled out his mobile phone. It beeped faintly, but there was no line out. Nicky cursed. The battery was flat.

He wondered for a moment about going to find someone, but it would be a battle going back through the crowd. And suppose the girl turned up? Suppose she was expecting him? She must have got him here for a reason. She might still want him to help her.

Outside there were footsteps. They seemed to stop, then move away. Nicky held his breath but nobody came in.

He shone the torch again, the beam glinting silver as it skimmed the metal door. It was open – just slightly – the thin black space of the doorway like a grim invitation to go through. And suddenly it made sense – whoever had taken Starlight had led her through there.

Nicky held back.

He remembered telling Billy he was stupid to go poking about in Chestnut Court. He remembered telling him that the place was a death-trap. He remembered Billy's stories about tunnels and cellars.

But then a picture of Starlight flashed into his head, and he knew he didn't have any choice.

32

Beyond the door the hallway narrowed and dipped steeply.

The torchlight shuddered against the yellow walls. The plaster was cracked and cratered where damp had seeped in behind it.

Nicky put his hands out. The building seemed to be squeezing in around him.

It was musty. Airless.

Nicky stumbled, missing the first of three stone steps and slipping awkwardly to the bottom. Panic caught him. He couldn't breathe. He couldn't think. The darkness behind him seemed as endless as the darkness ahead. He couldn't even remember the way out. And suddenly the torchlight hit another door. And from behind the door there came a sound. The hollow sound of something heavy shifting on wood.

33

Nicky pushed at the door. It cracked open like something in a horror video. Nicky waited for the hand on his shoulder. The ghostly laugh. The body swinging from the ceiling.

But instead he saw Starlight.

She was standing quietly, her head turned towards him. A swirl of glitter sparkled round her like fairy lights, making her magical. Enchanted. And then Nicky realized the glitter was really thick particles of dust caught in the beam of his torch.

Starlight was tethered to a crusted metal pipe that ran down from the ceiling. The wall was cracked. There were great gaping splits in the brickwork and most of the mortar had crumbled away. All the fear for himself faded and Nicky was beside her in two strides, cradling her head as he stroked her nose. "It's OK girl. I'll get you out. You'll be OK."

Starlight pressed up against him and whickered softly.

Nicky swung the torch beam round the cellar. He guessed from the length of the tunnel he'd just been down that he must be somewhere close to the derelict, forgotten corner that he'd discovered yesterday. The walls were a mass of crumbling pipes wrapped in rotted glass-fibre. Along one edge was a metal tank welded with more pipes, rusted valves and a cracked pressure gauge. It looked like an old water heating system.

Nicky moved the torch beam on. There was broken furniture stacked against the far wall. He picked out a chipped vase drooping with dusty silk flowers, a brass dancing horse with its front leg missing; a framed picture of a child with a star-shaped crack in the glass.

And then Nicky saw them. He stumbled backwards. The torch fell from his hand, rolling away with a dull rattle. The light from it snapped out like an eye closing.

But Nicky didn't need the light to hold on to what he'd seen. The image piled up in his mind. It was bodies. Soft, broken bodies heaped together like sacks. Their blond heads were all twisted. Their arms and legs were tangled together. Their blank empty eyes stared past him through the shadows.

34

Nicky pressed close to Starlight. She moved and snorted, pulling backwards against the pipe so that it clanked and echoed against the wall.

The dark pressed in.

Nicky battled to get a grip on himself. They were only dummies – the broken Levi Buick dummies that Suzy had told him about that day in the props trailer. The main thing was to untie Starlight – get them both out of here. If she jerked too hard, the wrench on the pipes could bring the ceiling down. And if they got trapped, who would know they were here? Only one person. The person who had hidden Starlight. And it didn't seem likely to Nicky that they would be letting on.

He felt his way along Starlight's body, his hands

finding her halter and struggling with the rope. It was knotted tight and he fumbled, cursing.

Starlight jerked her head again. Nicky heard the fresh scatter of rust.

And then he heard something else. Something coming down the damp dark corridor. Footsteps.

Nicky strained his ears. Was it one person? Was it ten? Was it the phone-caller coming to help him? Was it a horsenapper coming to hurt Starlight?

The footsteps came nearer.

Nicky stumbled sideways, feeling his way along the edge of the wall. He had to find something to crouch behind – somewhere to stay hidden until he knew who it was.

His hand brushed something soft. The dummies. They made the biggest mound in the room. It was the safest place to be. Nicky scrabbled, then dived amongst them, tangling his body with theirs. They dropped over him and around him. Nicky wriggled into position, one limp arm swinging down across his face. He closed his eyes. Playing dead.

35

It was a child's voice. A girl. It sounded strangely familiar, but Nicky couldn't put a face to it. He wished he could look, but he didn't dare. She was bound to have brought a torch or something with her, and at any moment she might search the cellar. The tiniest twitch could give him away.

He had to wait.

"I know he'll come." The voice came from over near Starlight. "He'll be looking for you. I've made it easy for him to guess where you are."

Nicky heard Starlight snort softly. At least she sounded OK.

"He won't be cross with me – not when he knows the truth," the girl's voice murmured on. "He'll be glad. He'll see I've come back at last."

Nicky's back was beginning to ache. Broken wire in the dummies pushed out through the soft foam, pressing into him. It hurt. The stale air was choking him. He gritted his teeth, trying to push down a new wave of panic. He wanted out of here. He couldn't take this much longer. And she was only a girl. She sounded young. Sabrina's age. Even if she got funny he could probably handle a girl like that.

Suddenly, above him, something shifted. There was the creak and rustle of something pressing on polystyrene. Nicky's heart lurched. He pulled his mouth tight, battling to stop himself from crying out. One of the dummies was *moving*.

And then something brushed his face. It felt very soft. It moved across him, catching at the flopping Levi Buick fringe of the dummy nearest to Nicky. The creaking stopped and there was a soft rumbling, like a tiny vibration. Then Nicky felt the pressure on him spring away. And suddenly Nicky remembered where he had felt that soft vibration before. He knew what it was that was slinking across him – and he knew who was in the cellar.

He opened his eyes slowly.

Three pairs of green, slanted eyes stared back. Elinora's cats.

He looked across the room. A paraffin lantern with purple glass was hanging from a jutting edge of pipe, throwing a coloured spotlight that dazzled and danced, lighting the cellar like a fairy grotto. And in that spotlight he saw Elinora's dark head buried deep in Starlight's mane.

So now he knew who.

He just didn't know why.

Up above him, the top dummy wobbled and slipped forward. Then slowly, with a sound like dead leaves rustling, the whole pile began to slide, tumbling across each other like children rolling down a hill.

36

Elinora sprang back, her eyes wide and startled as a cat's. Then she smiled. A child's smile. Warm and innocent. "I knew you'd come."

Nicky pushed the last of the dummies away from him. It slumped to the ground and he stepped over it, hearing the scrunch of polystyrene as he caught its arm with the edge of his trainer. "What's going on?"

Elinora twirled a strand of hair round her finger. "We can tell Dad everything. It'll be all right."

Nicky shook his head. He couldn't work her out. "Do you know Dad?"

"I've been waiting a long time."

Nicky didn't have a clue what she was talking about. Did she mean she'd been waiting with

Starlight? She made it sound like she'd been down here years, but he hadn't left Starlight until after five that afternoon. She couldn't have been here for more than four hours.

She stretched one arm out to him and took a step forward. "Joe..."

Nicky shook his head. Joe was Dad's name — so she must know Dad. He let his mind run back over all of Dad's mates. Gypsies they'd travelled with. Gorgios they'd worked with.

She came closer, her hand reaching out to him, gripping his wrist. The lantern lit her strangely, touching her hair with a purple glow. Her lips seemed to tremble suddenly, as if she was struggling not to cry. "Why didn't any of you come and get me after I got better? The social worker said it was for the best. She said Dad was a bad parent. But I didn't believe her. Dad was *never* a bad parent. And I've been waiting and waiting for one of you to come back for me ... only you never did..."

Nicky swallowed hard, trying to breathe slowly as he looked at her. Her eyes seemed glazed and distant. As Nicky watched her he wasn't sure who it was she was seeing. He said her name softly, rolling it over and over as he tried to puzzle her out. "Elinora Moon. Elinora. Elinora. Elinor. Elinor..." He stopped suddenly. His throat tightened. Tiny pulses of fear shivered up and down his back like insects under his skin. "Elinor. Ellie. Ellie Ghiselli. Dad's sister."

She smiled at him slowly. "We'll all be together again. It's going to be all right."

Nicky shook his head, trying to step backwards. Her grip tightened. She was stronger than he'd thought. "You're not Ellie. You can't be Ellie. Ellie's—" Nicky wanted to run, but he was sucked into the horror of what she was telling him. Ellie's accident had been rammed down his throat since before he could talk. It had been in the thick of every crappy, disastrous decision Dad made. But then – it had always been Ellie's *accident* – no one had ever said that she'd...

She was watching him carefully. "It'll be all right won't it? You won't leave me ever again?"

The word "ever" tolled like a bell. "What do you want from me?"

"I have to go back up soon," she whispered. "The other Elinora's waiting for me. She doesn't know that I planned all this. She's not always easy to talk to. But she misses you, and when I tell her you're waiting down here she'll *have* to listen to me. We'll go away – you, me and Starlight. Dad will come later. Elinora will bring him."

Nicky was shaking all over. He could smell his own sweat. "But you *are* Elinora. I don't know what happened. I know there was an accident – maybe you got hurt in the head. Maybe you're still not well..."

She didn't seem to be listening. "I've been waiting for you," she whispered. "I knew you'd come."

Nicky struggled to think straight. He could see she was nuts, but she wasn't stupid. She might be Sabrina's age at the moment, but she'd got Starlight down here. In her screwed-up, messed-up head she'd still managed all this. He could twist away from her and make a run for it, but that would mean leaving Starlight with her. Suppose she was dangerous? Suppose she tried to hurt Starlight to get back at him. He couldn't take the risk. He had to play for time – let her think he was going along with it all. "So what's the plan?"

"You'll have to stay down here – just for a little while. Just until everyone's gone away."

Nicky's thoughts were spinning. The walls of the cellar seemed to be closing in. "But what about Starlight?" He tried to keep his voice steady. "She'll need food. She'll need air..."

"It'll just be for a little while. Elinora will tell me when to let you out."

"But – what if something goes wrong?"

"We have to trust Elinora. I'm sure she won't let anything go wrong. She might be a bit worried, because she doesn't think it's safe down here, but that will make her act faster."

"How will you tell her?" Nicky couldn't get a grip on any of this. Ellie seemed to know Elinora, but did Elinora know Ellie.

She wrinkled her nose for a moment, puzzling it through. "Sometimes, if I concentrate very hard, I can make her notice me. But..." her voice dropped suddenly, thick with sadness, "she doesn't like thinking about me. It hurts her head, and it frightens her. She tries to push me away."

Nicky shook his head. He couldn't grasp what she was telling him, but he knew she was nuts. That was about as much as he could get a hold on for now. Making sense of it would have to wait until later. "What – what will she be able to tell other people?"

"I've worked it all out. She'll tell them she saw Starlight being driven away. She'll tell them you were there too. They'll believe that. You're a Gypsy boy. It's what they'd expect." She giggled suddenly, her head thrown back and her eyes starry-bright. A child with a secret. "Nobody will think to look in here. You'll be very safe."

"But – there's props down here. Surely the film crew will want..."

"It's all old stuff. It's just down here to keep it out of the way. And I heard Elinora tell someone this building's being knocked down soon. Anything left will just get crushed when the bulldozers come."

"But – suppose me and Starlight are still down here then?"

He watched her shake her head, as if this was something she hadn't thought about. It was a moment before she answered. "I'll try really, really hard to make her listen to me."

Nicky was growing colder and colder. The words *I'll try really, really hard* didn't sound all that promising.

And that row with Dad. Dad would think he'd run off again. Nicky had done it before. He'd gone to Grandad. Maybe this time Dad wouldn't be bothered. Maybe this time he wouldn't even want him back. And never in his life had Nicky wanted to be back home in that trailer more than he did now. His voice was beginning to shake. "And supposing it all goes OK – once it's safe for us to come out – where will you ask Elinora to take us?"

"Elinora's got lots of money. Elinora can sort things out. We'll have new names. A new look. And once Dad comes it'll be just like it used to be. We'll travel around. It's easy for Gypsies to disappear. We can have a new beginning, only with Elinora looking after us. Like a Fairy Godmother." She seemed to sway slightly, her eyes soft and dreamy, as if she was looking ahead to some magical time.

Nicky saw his chance. He twisted forward, pushing her sideways.

She clung to him, her fingers biting deep into his arm, and screamed.

And as she screamed the door pushed open.

It was Levi Buick.

37

"**W**hat the hell are you doing?"

Nicky saw the change in Elinora like a mask pulled down suddenly across her face. Slipping between time like a cat between shadows. She seemed dazed, shaking her head slightly, as if she'd been woken from a deep sleep. "I wanted to see Starlight. I – I think I was worried about her, with all the noise." She glanced at Nicky as if something was bothering her, but she couldn't quite pick out what it was.

Levi nodded. "I was worried too. That's why I slipped away from the hotel. I found the horse gone, and the fire door open. I sort of guessed the rest. But – what about you? What made you look down here?"

"I—" Elinora frowned, then pushed her hair

away from her face. "I – I wasn't well. The fireworks seemed to be exploding inside my head." She gave a nervous laugh. "I get terrible headaches sometimes. They get worse towards the end of a big shoot like this one. But," she turned to Nicky, "why are you here?"

"That was about to be my *next* question." Levi took a step nearer, and threw a stinging glance at Nicky. "It was a pretty dumb thing to do – stealing the horse and smuggling it down here. You can't have expected to get away with it."

Nicky shuffled awkwardly. What the hell could he say? He hadn't worked it out properly himself yet. The only thing he felt sure about was that Elinora Moon had a screw loose. "I found that fire-door open. I..."

"Did he try to hurt you?" Levi cut across Nicky's stumbling explanation.

Elinora covered her face with her hands, "No – of course not. My head was so bad, it's hard to remember..."

Nicky glanced at her. She really didn't know. Ellie and Elinora really *were* separate.

Levi looked round the cellar and whistled softly. "This place is the pits. I don't reckon we should hang around in here. We'll get Starlight out, and I'll call the cops." He narrowed his eyes at Nicky. "I guess I should have done that in the first place."

Levi picked his way past the broken props and muddle to Starlight. "Hey up." He slapped her neck as he went to unknot the halter. "Time for a scene change."

Nicky didn't quite see how it happened. Whether Starlight jumped back when Levi slapped her. Whether her foot caught on something as she moved towards him. Whatever it was, it panicked her. She half reared, twisting sideways. And as she pulled backwards there was the sound of splintering as the rusted metal broke away from its bracket. Hanging loose, it knocked against the wall, dislodging loose plaster that rattled to the ground like a fall of rocks. Starlight reared again. More pipes split away, this time tearing down from the ceiling. Elinora's lantern swayed madly on its hook, the purple light shuddering eerily.

And suddenly from above them there came a deep, low groan, like a dark monster waking.

Nicky didn't stop to think. He ran to Starlight, grabbing her halter. Levi had her too, holding tight to the other side. She plunged and kicked, a million years of instinct swamping a mere lifetime of training.

A child's voice screamed suddenly. "I'm scared, Joe. It's just like last time. She's going mad, the same as Midnight did!"

Nicky struggled to keep hold of Starlight. On the

other side of him Elinora was still screaming, making Starlight worse. He'd lose his grip in a minute. An idea flashed through him. If Elinora really *was* Dad's sister, perhaps he could reach her in her own world. It was worth a try. It might just work. "Get out of here Ellie. Go and get help."

"Starlight will hurt you. There'll be a pain in your head. A terrible, endless pain, just like there was for me. And they'll take you away. They'll say it was Dad's fault. I'll lose you both again. I should never have brought Starlight down here. I should have…"

Nicky glanced sideways at her as she talked. She was the child again, pale and scared. And she was sticking to the story. The whole idea was like something out of a horror film, but it still made sense in a sad, crazy sort of way.

Starlight plunged sideways. Her halter cut deep welts into his skin as he hung on to it. Once the side of her hoof caught his cheek with a stinging blow. On the other side of her Levi cursed and swore.

There wasn't much time.

Nicky had to make this work. "Ellie – listen to me. This is your chance to change everything. You won't lose me again if you do what I say. Go and get Elinora. Concentrate really hard. Tell her to ring Nicky's Dad. Tell her—" Nicky hesitated. "Tell her to make him understand who she is.

Maybe she can describe something that happened between them. Something hardly anyone else would know. Between them they'll make everything all right."

She stared back at Nicky. Her eyes were huge. Her face ghost-white with powdery dust.

"Go on. *Please!*"

Then she nodded, tears running in silent streams down her cheeks. With the three cats pressed close beside her she turned and disappeared through the door and into the black hole of the tunnel.

"What the hell's going on?" Levi battled with Nicky to bring Starlight down on to all four feet. "What does she mean – she just said *she* brought Starlight down here. I thought it was you."

"She just—" Nicky hesitated. This was no moment to announce there was a chance she was really Dad's little sister, looming up out of a tragic past that had left her more than a bit batty. "She said she wanted to get Starlight away from the fireworks."

"I think she's lost it," Levi muttered, breathing hard as Starlight jerked and twisted, trying to rear up again. "It happens sometimes, at the end of a shoot. It's all the pressure. The actors are still hyped up, but all the action's over. They just have to sit and wait until the film comes out. I reckon the adrenalin turns in on them. Makes them crazy."

The ceiling creaked again. A fresh fall of plaster spattered down. Nicky coughed. The dust choked him. His eyes were stinging. Full of grit.

Starlight plunged again, wrenching at his arm so that it ached.

Suddenly Elinora's lantern clattered to the floor. The small paraffin flame inside flickered and died.

Everything went black.

38

"What the hell do we do now?" Levi began to cough.

Nicky was coughing too. "I need five minutes with her. We have to get her to come quietly."

"Your Gypsy tricks would be fine if we had all day to play with them."

"The floor's rotted. There's pipes and plaster everywhere. If she struggles she'll fall."

"And what if the ceiling comes down while you're busy whispering sweet nothings in her ear?"

"You don't have to stay." Nicky could feel Levi glaring at him in the darkness. The stench of Levi's sweat mingled with his own. Both of them were still hanging fiercely on to Starlight's halter, and breathing hard. "Keep a straight line to the door. If you fall, don't swear too loud. She'll pick up on your mood."

There was a long silence.

The ceiling creaked again.

More plaster rattled down.

"I'm staying with the horse." Levi coughed again. "What d'you need me to do?"

"I'm going to start with stroking. You do that side, and I'll do this. We need big, slow movements that will settle her down."

"Just stroking?"

"It's more than stroking. Do it like you're swimming. Move from your shoulder."

Starlight felt tighter than stretched elastic. She shivered. Nicky brushed the dust from his eyes and pressed against her. He didn't hear the groans and creaks now. He didn't feel the ache in his arm. And it didn't matter that he couldn't see. He knew all Starlight's shapes and curves. He knew just where to touch.

After a moment Nicky felt the change. The colours were coming, softening from harsh reds to hazy greens and blues.

"How are you doing?" Nicky suddenly remembered Levi was there.

"My arm's killing me."

"You can stop now. We need to lean on her. You against that shoulder, me against this one."

"Why?"

"She'll pick up on our breathing. If we keep it steady she'll get a sense that there's nothing to worry about."

The ceiling creaked again.

Levi gave a dry laugh. "You reckon you can do that?"

"Pretend you've been given a script. Just act it."

It was a moment before Levi spoke again, "This feels weird. There's a kind of heat coming off her..."

"We'll risk walking her now. We'll let her guide us as much as she can. Horses are nocturnal. They see well in the dark—"

There was a sound like roaring. The roar grew thunderous. There was cracking. Splitting. "Get a firm hold of her head..." yelled Nicky.

"I can't," shouted Levi. "The floor's going away from me – oh hell— "

39

Everything hurt. Lumps of plaster struck Nicky's head. Shards of pipework cut into his legs. "Levi – are you OK?"

There was silence.

"Levi—?" Nicky's voice bounced, echoing round the room.

Suddenly he heard another groan – not a crumbling building now, but a human sound. "Hell – this hurts."

"What's happened?"

"My leg. It's gone through the floor. I can't move."

"Where are you?"

"How the hell should I know? In a black hole somewhere, I guess."

"Reach out your hand. I'm still with Starlight. See if you can touch her."

There was a moment's silence. "Got it."

"What bit d'you think you're near to?"

Another silence. "Belly, I think."

"OK. I'm going to try and move her forward." Nicky clicked his tongue, and Starlight took two paces with him. "Touch her again."

Two seconds later Levi gave a short laugh. "Thanks, pal. I've just got the horse's backside in my face."

"So can you feel her tail?"

"Yep."

"Get hold of it, and hang on tight. I'm taking her forward."

As Nicky touched her, Starlight stayed steady. She walked slowly, as if she suddenly knew it was her instead of them that was in charge. Nicky could hear splintering wood, and the sound of something heavy being dragged. He stopped. "Are you OK?"

"I'm hoping nobody's been feeding this horse baked beans."

"Just don't let go. I'm taking her forward again. I can't see where the hell we're heading, so I'm just keeping with Starlight."

"I wish I could be as certain of this horse as you are." Levi's voice was tense. Nicky knew he wouldn't let on, but he guessed Levi was in a lot of pain.

He lifted his hand up to Starlight's forehead, his fingers pressing lightly on the spot between her eyes, a message of trust sparking between them.

And as he touched her Nicky saw the door. He saw it clearly – not as a hole in the darkness, but with its frame, and the brick wall around it. Even the handle had a dull glow. And he could see more than that. He could pick out shapes in the cellar. Fallen beams. Bits of props. Up above him the cracks in the ceiling left jagged spaces like black stars. There was still no light. Nothing had changed. But Nicky felt a fresh burst of energy. He was seeing through Starlight's eyes again.

Suddenly, there *was* a light. A thin yellow beam searching the darkness. Nicky heard a voice calling, echoing through the tunnel. "Nicky? Nicky?" Heavy footsteps strode towards him. Strong arms grabbed him, holding him in a great bear-hug. There was the rasping sound of someone not used to crying. It was Dad.

40

They stumbled back up into Starlight's room.
It hadn't caved in like the cellar, but there
were long cracks in the plaster. The fireplace had
shifted slightly and the vases were broken. The
flowers lay in a bright scatter amongst the straw,
and down the wall ran a thin stain of water, like a
silver trail.

In the centre of the room the ceiling was sagging.
The chandelier swung dangerously, the crystals
tinkling and twittering like frightened birds.

"Keep going." Dad was behind Starlight now,
with Levi leaning and stumbling against him. "We
need to get right away from here."

Suddenly a figure appeared in the doorway. It
stood for a moment, huge and powerful. Strange

stripes of light glowed as it moved, heading for Nicky. "Is everyone OK?"

Nicky wiped his hand across his face, looking up at the fire-fighter. "I think so."

The fire-fighter touched Nicky's arm, and turned to Dad. "Is there anybody else trapped down there?"

Dad wiped away a thin stream of blood that was trickling down from his forehead, his other arm still steadying Levi. "No. Everybody's safe."

"Let's go then." The fire-fighter nodded at Nicky, and strode forwards to help Dad with Levi.

Nicky led them all out through the room and into the floodlit night.

41

Nicky stood with Starlight under a tree.
He was achingly tired. His head throbbed and
he guessed he'd be covered in bruises by morning.
But he'd checked Starlight over and she seemed
OK. Just a few bumps and scratches, and a cut on
her nose.

As he leant against her something fluttered,
rustling the leaves above him. Looking up, Nicky
saw a balloon – one of the gold metallic horse ones
– twisting and dancing with its string snagged on
one of the branches. Nicky wondered for a moment
about the child who had lost it.

In front of him Chestnut Court was cordoned off
with bright orange tape. The searchlights from the
fire engines lit the grounds brighter than daylight,

making it seem like a giant film set. In the centre of the action, the star performers were the fire-fighters. They towered above everyone, their uniforms flashing neon-bright stripes. Nicky watched them with a sense of wonder. They seemed to be like glowing defenders, guarding all the doors – an alien army keeping earthling reporters and photographers from danger.

An ambulance, its blue light flashing, screeched up and stopped near the marquee. Levi was there, being fussed over by Courtney and Suzy. Nicky watched as someone brought a wheelchair down the ramp. In spite of his aches he grinned to himself as Levi limped past it, leaning against Suzy instead. They were no more likely to get Levi in a wheelchair than they were to get him to agree to be driven around in a pick-up truck.

Courtney broke into Nicky's thoughts, hurrying over with a plastic cup full of water. "Has the doctor checked you over?" She handed the water to Nicky.

Nicky coughed, bending double as the icy fresh rush washed the grit from his throat. "I don't need her. It's only scratches and stuff. She's fussing with Dad at the moment. He got a gash on his head."

Courtney waved away a reporter, but couldn't stop a photographer flashing his camera in Nicky's face.

"Please let me get someone to look at you. I'm supposed to have taken care of you."

"I've had worse lumps and bumps than this before."

"It's my job to worry about you. I don't know if it's worth it. Tonight's been a complete nightmare. I'm thinking I might go back to nannying ... get a job with sweet pretty children whose biggest trauma is when one of them loses a ballet shoe." She gave Nicky a tired smile, squeezed his arm again and hurried back towards the ambulance.

"You OK?" Dad came towards him.

Nicky nodded. "Fine. Your cut's pretty deep though."

Dad shrugged. "They've cleaned it up. I've had worse."

"Yes, but – you ought to go to hospital. It might need stitches."

Dad raised his eyebrows. "I'll go if you go."

Nicky looked away. "I can't stand those places. You know I can't."

"Me neither."

They stood without speaking for a moment, and Nicky stole another glance at Dad. He looked strained. Shocked. Nicky pushed his fingers through Starlight's mane. Part of him wanted to leave Ellie – Elinora – whoever she was – in the past. But it was too big a secret. And she could still be a danger. He had to get this over with. "How – how did you know where to look for me?"

Dad closed his eyes and shook his head. "She rang me."

"You mean Elinora?"

There was a long silence. "Yes."

"So – what did she say?"

Dad clenched his fists. "I can't believe your Grandad would have..."

"She told you who she was?"

"Yes."

"And didn't you believe her?" Nicky spoke softly, his eyes meeting Dad's.

"I didn't want to. I wanted her to be a fraud. It was too much to take in. But – she knew about Midnight. That was the name of the horse that hurt Ellie. There's hardly anyone else in the world who would have remembered that."

"So—" Nicky looked away. This was bad enough for him. It must be like a nightmare for Dad. "You think she *might* really be Ellie?"

"It's been going round in my mind since I got you safe. Loads of questions – things I've always tried not to think about. There wasn't a funeral, and I never asked why. I was too wrecked to really think about it. Afterwards, Grandad just clammed up the couple of times I tried to ask, so I just pushed it away. I thought he didn't want to dig up old griefs. But..."

"But what, Dad?" Nicky had to keep him talking. It would be too easy to let it all get buried again.

"There was no grave either. There should have been a grave for us to visit." Dad rubbed the back of his hand across his eyes, then stood staring across towards the fire-fighters.

Nicky suddenly wanted to pull him back into the present. "So – what else did Elinora say?"

"Not much. There wasn't time. She was shouting – telling me you were in trouble. I just jumped in the pick-up and raced over here. The other stuff's only just beginning to hit me."

Nicky laid his arm on Dad's wrist. "She told me stuff too – while I was down in the cellar. It was her who took Starlight in there. And – if she *is* Ellie then she's ill – really sick in the head."

Dad punched his fist suddenly into the air. "But how could Grandad could have done that to her? Or to me?"

Nicky gripped Dad's arm tighter. "Wait till you've spoken to him. Wait till you know his side."

"I don't think I'll ever..."

Richard King appeared suddenly with a security guard. "We've got a stable ready for Starlight, in the old block where they used to keep the carriage horses. This is Bill – he's going to be with her all night. In the morning we'll move her on to somewhere more secure."

"So –" Nicky turned to Richard King, wondering how much *he* knew – "who d'you think tried to take her?"

"There's always loads of weirdos that hang around a film set. It wasn't anyone very organized. She was too easy to find. The papers are already taking the line that we were pulling some kind of publicity stunt." Richard King shook his head irritably. "As if we would have the time to set that up." His yellow eyes flicked across Nicky. "Do you know anything then? Did you see anything odd?"

Nicky hesitated. He should probably tell Richard King everything. He should probably tell the gavvers – get the law involved. Elinora was sick. She needed help. But she was Gypsy too – and Gypsies don't tell each other's secrets to the gorgios. This was something between him and Dad and Grandad.

Bill the security guard took Starlight's halter. "I'll take her round. I know about horses. I do this sort of thing for the big racing stables all the time."

Nicky watched Starlight go, a flurry of flashlights going off again as she was led past the photographers. She wasn't bothered, just looking round at them with her dark beautiful eyes. She'd seen it all before.

As she disappeared round the corner Nicky turned back to Dad.

He was shocked at how sunken and old and lost he looked.

"I want to go home," said Dad suddenly.

They walked together back towards the pick-up. Dad trailed slightly behind. "Come on." Nicky turned to him gently. "Keep up." It struck him as he said it that he was sounding like the adult, and Dad was the child.

42

Elinora appeared like a ghost from round the side of the pick-up. The cats were with her, their eyes glowing in the shadowy darkness.

"Joe —"

"Ellie?"

Nicky stared at her. Who was she now — the woman or the girl?

There was an endless silence. It was Elinora who broke it. "I'm sorry."

"Is it really you, Ellie? I didn't believe..." Dad left the sentence unfinished. "If I'd known I would have tried to find you —"

"Maybe that's why our dad did what he did. Maybe he couldn't face putting you through any more pain."

Nicky relaxed slightly. She was definitely the woman.

"How can you say that?" Dad's voice exploded. "How can you say that thinking you were dead would have been better than knowing you were alive?"

"Think about it, Joe. Dad was trapped. Social Services had him down as a 'bad parent'. They put me with foster parents – gorgio families. No one was ever unkind…"

"He should have fought for you. He should have dug trenches with his bare hands. Climbed mountains. Whatever he had to do." Dad glanced sideways at Nicky. "That's what I would have done."

"We were Gypsies, Joe, and times were different then. As far as any court was concerned, we were already tainted. Dad would always have lost. And maybe he thought it was for the best. I was ill for a long time – in and out of hospital. I had to learn to walk again, do up buttons, even manage the toilet… How could Dad have coped with all that?"

"How can you be so forgiving? So – so damned *grown-up*!"

"I've had most of my life to think it all through. And there was something else – another worry for him."

"What was that?" Dad was walking up and

down, almost stumbling, as if the wind was buffeting him.

"You." Elinora's hair whipped across her face. "If he'd tried too hard to get me back, they might have turned on him more sharply. He might have lost you as well. I don't suppose you know, but at the time he was being hounded by the press – gorgio reports saying Gypsies let their kids run wild. Gorgio reports saying Gypsies let their kids dabble with danger. A couple of babies were taken away from other Gypsy families at the time, because of stupid things that got blown up by all the fuss. There was a kind of madness going on."

Dad stopped walking and spun to face her. "How do you know all this?"

"When I was about to leave home – a gorgio foster home – I got a really good social worker. Someone who really understood. At the time I'd wanted to find you all again, and she said she'd help me. She made enquiries – found out where you were."

"So why didn't you come then?" Dad sounded choked.

"Because she'd been asking around – very discreetly – and found out that everyone thought I was dead. I had to make a choice."

"So you chose to stay away?"

Nicky could hear the pain in Dad's voice, but

Elinora's view made a sort of sense. If it happened to him, what would he do? Would he churn up Sabrina's world like that? And he understood Grandad too. He remembered once Grandad telling him that the past could weigh you down for ever, if you let it. Nicky was sure letting Ellie go would have broken Grandad's heart, but he must have believed it was for the best.

"I'd changed so much." Elinora's words tumbled out, as if she was desperate to explain. "I could never have fitted back in. I was even scared of horses. I didn't know if Dad would be able to cope with that. Cats were as much as I could manage. But I had other things happening to me at about that time too. I was pretty, I was bright, and I got myself noticed. A film producer spotted me. He did a screen test, and signed me up. It was a new beginning. A way of putting the past behind me." She sighed. "And I was good at acting. Good at being somebody else. I suppose it was because I'd lost who I really was, so I could just keep re-inventing myself."

"Was *The Other Side of Heaven* harder because you were playing a Gypsy?" Nicky spoke for the first time. He was desperate to find out what was going on in her head – what she was likely to do next, and what she remembered about tonight.

Elinora turned to him. "It frightened me. Some

of the bits were so close to my own life. I nearly turned it down when I first played the tape. I get all my scripts on tape – I've never learnt to read properly, although I've never told anyone about that – until now." She gave him a tired smile and shrugged. "Anyway – I'm getting older. A middle-aged actress doesn't get so many parts offered. I was scared that if I didn't do this one, I might not get anything else for ages."

"And did playing a Gypsy make you –" Nicky stopped, struggling to choose the right words. "Did it sort of bring everything back?"

"Not at first. I thought I was coping. I thought I was professional enough just to treat it like another job." Elinora paused, her voice softening suddenly. "And then I saw you, last Friday afternoon, in the field with Levi. It was weird. I was so drawn to you. I found out who you were – and then you turned up on the set. It knocked me sideways. All the old pain came flooding back."

"So, do you think seeing me might have – well, dug up too many old memories. Messed you up somehow?"

Elinora frowned. "For years I'd always had odd things happen to me. Headaches. Black-outs. Times when I'd come round and find myself in the middle of something really strange, like doing a kid's drawing, or cuddling a toy that I didn't even remember buying. I've had that more than ever this week. It's – it's frightened me."

The wind gusted suddenly, and Nicky shivered. "Do you remember about this evening? Do you remember about being with Starlight?"

Elinora shook her head. "It's all like a dream. The sort of nightmare where you can remember the terror, but not what actually happened."

"You – you took Starlight down to the cellar," Nicky said quietly.

"Why did I do that?" Elinora looked startled. Scared.

"You wanted to get me to go looking for her. You thought I was Dad. You wanted us all to get back together again."

Elinora pushed her head into her hands and stood for a moment, swaying like a tree in the wind. "I'm so sorry." Her voice dropped to a whisper. "I just remember being in Starlight's room. It was very dark. Starlight wasn't there and I had this terrible sense of dread. Then this little girl began screaming at me. Telling me to get help. I couldn't see her but I could hear her, and I thought I knew her voice. I struggled to work out who she was but I couldn't remember her name. I think she ran off because everything suddenly went quiet. It was then that I rang Joe..." Elinora reached out to touch him, then dropped her arm down suddenly. "I'm going away tonight. A special clinic. I spoke to my doctor just now, and she recommends it."

Dad didn't seem to have been listening to them. He was walking up and down again. "You're coming back with us now, aren't you? We can't leave it like this."

"I'll stay in touch. I'll let you know where I am. But –" Elinora smiled sadly – "I won't come back. Not to the old life. I am who I've become. But – I'm glad I've seen you. And I'm glad I've met Nicky. He's got a magic gift with horses. He's like I would have been. I wish I could have done something for him..." She let the sentence fade. Instead she reached out to Dad, and this time she didn't drop her hand back. Their fingers linked awkwardly, holding tight for a moment. "Don't worry about me," she said softly. "I've got this far on my own. I know I'll get through the next bit." Then she turned and walked away.

Nicky and Dad watched until she and the cats had disappeared back into the darkness, then turned towards the pick-up.

"Are you OK?" Nicky said.

Dad pulled his hands through his hair. He shook his head. He pulled at his eyes with his fingers. "I'm not great," he said at last. "But I'm better than I thought I'd be."

Nicky nodded and climbed into the front seat of the pick-up.

As Dad reversed, Nicky glanced back towards Chestnut Court.

The wind was gusting again, shaking the last leaves from the trees. Suddenly Nicky saw the golden-horse balloon break free from the branch and go whirling away, spinning and twisting across the night until it was just a tiny dark dot in the distance.

43

Nicky ran his fingers through Starlight's mane. She turned and blew gently on his shoulder. He buried his head deep into her, wishing he could somehow close himself round her and never let her go.

Dad had dropped Nicky at Chestnut Court after lunch. He was collecting his new pick-up that afternoon, and Nicky thought he'd want him to go too. But when Nicky had asked if he could spend the last few hours with Starlight, Dad had just offered to drive him there on his way to the garage. He'd been quiet all morning. He'd told Mum and Sabrina a bit of what had gone on, but he'd refused to ring Grandad. When Nicky offered to do it instead, he'd bitten his head off.

Outside Starlight's stable Nicky heard the security guard talking. "Just stick them here. We'll load them in a lorry later."

Nicky didn't bother to look out. He guessed it was another florist's delivery. Since the news of last night had leaked out there'd been a stream of vans bringing anything from tiny posies to huge bursting bouquets.

At least Starlight seemed well. He'd checked her over for pain, or signs of shock, but she was fine – just a bit of tension on her hindquarters around her tail.

"You look like you've been in a fight."

Nicky looked round, touched his bruised cheek, and grinned. "You look like you've been in ten."

"My foot's blown up like a balloon." Levi grinned back. "But remember the rest could all be make-up with me. I might not want everyone to think you suffered more than I did."

"Typical actor. Never wants to be upstaged." Bretta appeared, nudging Levi as he hung over the stable door. She was smiling too, but she didn't fool Nicky. Her pale, drawn face was like a reflection of his own. Levi was going today as well.

"So – how come there's not hundreds of sobbing fans hanging round you?" Nicky stroked Starlight's neck, trying to push down the rush of sadness that washed over him. He'd had his last moments on his own with her. He'd have to play it light from now on.

"There's hundreds of girls camped out at the hotel. Except I didn't stay there. Courtney organized a 'secret hideaway'. I got driven here this morning in a rusted-up pick-up truck. Courtney wasn't keen on me coming at all, but I wanted to check on the horse and – I guessed you'd be here."

Nicky met his look. He felt awkward suddenly. He hadn't even tried to get to know the bloke. If he hadn't been such a prat all week they might have got on. They might have had a laugh. "I – it was good you were there last night. I would never have held Starlight on her own."

"Me neither." Levi flicked a flake of wood off the stable door and looked away. "What you do with horses is—"

Suddenly there was the sound of an engine. A horse trailer was backing up round the corner.

Nicky felt pain like a ton of bricks crushing against his chest.

"Do you want to lead her in?" Levi unbolted the door and hobbled backwards.

Nicky put his hand up to Starlight's halter. She had arched her neck, and was looking towards the silver and gold horsebox with her ears pricked forward. "Looks like she's ready for it." His voice sounded gruff. Like it was full of gravel.

Levi glanced sideways at Bretta. "It's part of the life. It's the same for all of us in the business. We keep moving on." He went as if to slap Starlight's neck, and then stopped. Instead he ran his hand along her very slowly, turned to Nicky and grinned. "I've got to imagine I'm swimming, right? Take it from the shoulder?"

Nicky nodded, but he couldn't bring himself to speak. Instead he touched Starlight's forehead. She whickered softly, but her dark eyes strained towards the horsebox. He suddenly held out the halter rope to Levi. "Here – you take her."

Levi took the rope.

"It's been good knowing you." Levi clapped Nicky on the back.

"Watch it." Nicky forced a grin. "Your bruises might be all make-up, but mine aren't."

"Sorry pal." Levi winked at him. "Maybe I'll see you at the film preview?"

"Maybe." Nicky stood for a moment, watching the autumn sun touch Starlight with shimmers of gold as she followed Levi into the horsebox.

Nicky raised his hand briefly, nodded at Bretta, then walked quickly away.

44

Bretta walked towards Nicky as he stood in the field, kicking through the last fall of leaves under the chestnut tree. "Are you OK?"

"Great." Nicky looked at her pale blotchy face and puffed-up eyes. "How about you?"

"Great."

"So – they've gone then?"

"Levi's limo came five minutes after Starlight went off. He offered me a lift but – it's better like this."

She turned and looked back towards Chestnut Court. "You can't see all the tapes and warnings from here, can you? You can't see that the place is really a death-trap."

Nicky followed her gaze. It was all still beautiful.

The walls still caught the gold of the late-afternoon sun, so that the whole place glowed and glittered like a palace in a fairy-tale. "I guess that's what makes it so dangerous," he said.

They were quiet for a moment.

Suddenly Nicky reached up and pulled at a low hanging branch from the tree, twisting down a conker still half in its shell. He split the spiky case open and held the conker between his fingers, squinting at it with one eye. "What are you going to do now?"

Bretta sighed. "Get back to the real world, I s'pose. How about you?"

"About the same, I guess." He hurled the conker away. It flew long and high, a small red dot skimming off into the distance.

Bretta whistled. "That was good." She reached up suddenly, twisting down a conker from another branch, and giggled. "Can you teach me that?"

45

"I've had some wonderful news." Maddy hurried towards Nicky as he pushed open the gate at the bottom of her garden.

Dusty looked up from grazing in a patch of thistles, and wandered over to them.

Nicky rubbed Dusty's ears and turned back to Maddy. "What's happened?"

"A woman from a children's TV programme called *Crazy About Creatures* just rang me. They saw Dusty with you on the news last Sunday, and contacted the publicity people at Chestnut Court to find out more about him. When I told her his background she got more and more excited. She wants to do a piece on him – sort of following his progress. They'll pay for his keep – and she reckoned there'll be donations sent in by viewers too. It means I can afford to keep him – and probably a few more like him as well."

"That's really great." Nicky stood facing her as the long shadows of the fading afternoon stretched across the garden. It *was* good news. He was really pleased for her. But he felt fed-up too. Nothing had really changed at home. It wouldn't be any easier getting to work with the new donkeys than it had been working with Dusty.

They both looked round at the sound of an engine. Nicky's heart sank as he saw Dad's old pick-up pull up at the side of the house. He was supposed to have gone straight home after he'd said goodbye to Starlight.

Maddy saw Nicky's expression. "Do you want me to talk to him?"

Nicky shook his head. "I'll be better on my own."

As Maddy hurried off, Dad walked across the garden to Nicky. "I've been expecting you back at the site. Mum's doing burgers and baked tatties."

"I – I was just about to leave." Nicky scratched Dusty's neck and looked away. "I thought you were getting the new pick-up today."

"I changed my mind. It's not the most important thing at the moment."

"Why? What else has broken?"

Dad gave him a long, slow look. "I've been on the phone all afternoon."

Nicky met the look. "Talking to Grandad?"

"Some of the time."

"So – what's he say?" Nicky got a picture of Grandad in his head. His weathered brown face. His old felt hat. They'd always been so close.

"He hung up at first. Wouldn't talk about it. Then he rang back."

Nicky nodded. Grandad would do that. "What did he say?"

"It's all true. Everything. And he's going through hell now."

Nicky turned away suddenly. "So – is that what you wanted? To put him through hell?" Grandad had made a mess of things – Nicky knew that – but was the past going to go on and on hurting them all for ever?

Dad looked at Nicky for a long time without speaking, then said slowly, "You're wrong. Your Grandad's a good bloke. I don't like what he did – I don't think he was right – but he did it for the best reasons. And they lied to him too. The social workers told him Ellie would never get properly better. They told him she wouldn't be much more than a vegetable for the rest of her life. And I think, when he heard that, your Grandad wished she *was* dead. He told me never a day went by without him having to think of her strapped in some hospital bed, on drips and stuff, hour after hour after hour."

"So," Nicky leant against Dusty, "what's going to happen now?"

"We've both agreed to get a message to Ellie. If she wants to contact him again, he'll be waiting. If she doesn't, well, he reckons he'll just have to live with whatever she chooses."

Nicky nodded. It was odd hearing Dad talk about Grandad like that. It was odd hearing about them agreeing on things. They'd been at each other's throats for as long as he could remember. "So – what was the other stuff? The reason why you're not getting a new pick-up?"

"When I'd finished talking to Grandad the phone went again. In fact it hasn't stopped all afternoon. It's been going crazy."

Nicky stiffened suddenly. Perhaps Elinora had slipped back to being Ellie making strange phone calls again. "Who – who was it?"

"All sorts. Riding schools. Stud farms. Kids with horses that buck, rear, won't go in horseboxes, won't come out of horseboxes. You name it, I've heard about it today."

"So," Nicky was only half listening as the relief that it wasn't Ellie settled round him, "what did they want to know?"

"They want to talk to you. Ask you things.

Apparently that Levi Buick bloke was interviewed on telly at lunchtime and said how you calmed Starlight down and everything..."

Nicky shrugged and turned away, untangling an imaginary knot in Dusty's mane. There wasn't much point even thinking about all these hundreds of horses and their owners. He'd be back cutting trees with Dad and Jim next weekend.

"...And that's why I'm not getting a new pick-up. We're going to need to use that money for something else."

"How d'you mean?"

"This gift that Ellie was talking about – this horse magic – it seems a shame to waste it." Dad cleared his throat loudly. "And let's face it – keeping you away from horses has never really got us very far."

Nicky tried to push back the excitement that was blowing through him. What was Dad saying?

"And – if I'm going to let you go off sorting out other people's horses, you're going to need something to get there on. I won't have time to drive you all over the place."

A picture of a bike came into Nicky's mind. He'd need something that would go through fields and stuff easily. And as he thought about it, he felt a fresh rush of energy. Working with horses. Troubled horses. Difficult horses. Being allowed to spend time with them, and their owners. To be a real horse healer. He turned to Dad, grinning, for the first time. "A mountain bike would be good."

"That wasn't what I had in mind," Dad said slowly.

Nicky shrugged. It didn't matter too much what it was. "It doesn't need to be new. I've seen them in the newsagent's window. You can get them for a good price if you wait for the right one."

Dad shook his head and looked straight at Nicky. "I thought a horse would be better."

Nicky turned away and looked across the field.

It was dusky light. The first evening star was out, glittering above Chestnut Court. Nicky stared at it for a long time, but he couldn't see it properly. It was blurry. Out of focus. Nicky blinked twice, and brushed his arm fiercely across his eyes. Other stars were coming now, like tiny lights switching on one by one. For some crazy reason he started to count them, but it was impossible. There were too many. Thousands and thousands. All that mystery. All that past. And all that future.

"Nicky?" Dad sounded clumsy and uncertain, his voice reaching Nicky from a strange, dizzying distance. "I said, a horse would be better – wouldn't it?"

Nicky swallowed hard, then turned and looked at Dad at last. "A horse would be great," he said.

**Have you read the
first book in the series?**

Horse
Healer

Eclipse

1

Every time he went, Nicky knew he was doing something wrong. If he ever got caught, he'd really be for it. Except it didn't *feel* wrong. Not in his heart. It was just that he knew that no one else would ever see it in the same way he did.

He slowed his bike to a halt and wheeled it silently into the bushes, wedging it inside a tangle of brambles so it couldn't be seen from the road.

A black car was coming, travelling fast down the country lane. Nicky ducked down out of sight and waited as it roared past.

As the growl of the engine faded into the distance, Nicky straightened up. Stepping softly out into the open, he vaulted lightly across the five-barred gate. He made no sound as he landed.

Quietly, very quietly, he crept between the cluster of trees that lined the edge of the field.

It was dusk, and already shapes and shadows were beginning to spread towards each other across the silence. The moon was out, but its silver crescent was masked behind heavy grey clouds.

In the dusty half-light Nicky could still make out the horse grazing at the far side of the field. Eclipse, an Arab mare, with a coat so dark that in some lights she looked completely black. She had no other markings except for a partial star on her forehead. And she was beautiful. Nicky loved all horses, but she was something above the others. There was a magic about her, a wildness that drew him to her again and again.

He stood for a long time, letting the darkness settle around him, listening to scratchings and scrabblings that rustled the leaves of the whispering trees.

Nearby a twig snapped. Nicky tensed, his sharp green eyes darting towards the sound. It was only a squirrel scuttering up a nearby tree.

Nicky took a deep breath. He felt odd tonight. Jumpy. But he was stupid to feel jumpy. The night would be spoilt if he was on edge. And he didn't want it spoilt. It was too precious. Too special. He was hungry for the buzz of excitement and the racing energy that Eclipse always gave him.

He stepped forward and, low in his throat, he uttered a call. It was a deep, almost animal sound.

Immediately Eclipse lifted her head, her ears flicking forward as she listened.

Nicky called again and Eclipse began to trot towards him, whickering softly.

She drew up close and for a moment they just stood, watching each other. There was no fear between them. Nicky knew Eclipse and Eclipse knew Nicky. He held out his hand and she nuzzled against him. She wasn't looking for treats or tit-bits. Her action was a simple greeting. A warm welcome.

Nicky touched the half-star on her forehead. It was a light movement, very gentle, but Eclipse understood it. It was a sign – a secret message to reassure her, and to strengthen the trust between them. Then he moved to her side. He ran his hand along her neck and shoulder, then leaned against her, catching the rich, sweet smell of her body.

He sprang up on to her.

He didn't kick, or even push with his knees, and although his hands touched the rich silk of her mane, he didn't hold on.

"Walk." He spoke gently, almost whispering, yet Eclipse responded immediately, arching her neck and stepping out proudly as she moved forwards. This was the moment Nicky always loved best, the moving together as if they were almost one animal.

"Now trot." Squeezing with his legs, Nicky guided Eclipse round in a perfect figure of eight, first one way, and then the other. A quiet word made her stop instantly, her nostrils flared and her neck arched. Another squeeze and she was cantering, moving like a dream horse, with a floating grace that had a magic all of its own.